INSP

(26 Southern, Red-clay-stained stories of Inspiration)

by

Steven Ray Bowen

Artwork by Steve Smith

To Ann -
May the Lord
bless you! I hope
you enjoy the book!
[signature]

First published by Dog Ear Publishing
4010 W. 86th Street, Ste H
Indianapolis, IN 46268
www.dogearpublishing.net

ISBN: 978-159858-265-9
Library of Congress Control Number: 2006939663

This book is printed on acid-free paper.

Printed in the United States of America

ACKNOWLEDGMENTS

Ah, I owe many thanks to more than a few people who offered roadside assistance to me on this journey:

To the early readers of the manuscript: Mary Massad, Janet Counts, and Leota Laster. Leota, a loyal reader of my work for years, did much in particular in assuring me that the selection of stories and the order were good. Plus she did my final read through, so if you see any mistakes, let her know!

To Marsha Esquivel, who read the manuscript and built up my confidence with her spirited and enthusiastic response to the work. Marsha's boost of confidence was important, because my friend Jean Hisle came right behind her with a mean eye and shot down some of my minor slipups that had holed up in the manuscript.

To Laurie Magers, Zig Ziglar's assistant, who read *Inspiration Point* before she ever met me and loved it. She's been a big supporter through this process and did extensive proofreading and editing for me in the final stages.

To my excellent artist, Steve Smith, who read the manuscript and drew what he saw. For those of you who like to look at the pictures, you're in luck.

To my family, who has long had to live with a dreamer.

And, especially, thanks to all of my readers through the years, who read the newspaper stories and the e-mails and who buy the books, helping me keep making people laugh and cry on a pretty regular basis.

Many of the stories you're about to read appeared in similar form as you'll find here between 1997 and 2003 in my weekly Saturday morning newspaper column in the *La Grange Daily News* in La Grange, Georgia. That is where many of us first met. The dates at the end of each story signify when the story was originally written and published.

sb

Remembering Grandma, who once said reading my column in the paper each week was like getting a letter from home...

INSPIRATION POINTS

(Contents)

FOREWARNING

(The trip up Inspiration Point could pull your heartstrings or cause sharp pain in your side from laughter, so please read this Forewarning before beginning the climb.)

There is no *serious* warning to offer you as you begin reading "Inspiration Point," but I should at least alert you that you might need a tissue handy when you pick up this book to read—that is, if you happen to be the sensitive, emotional type. As most ladies know, we men are pretty much immune to being that sentimental. The worst that happens to us while we're reading a tearjerker is maybe we'll have something in the air irritate our eyes and give us the sniffles. Other than that, we're pretty much made of steel.

And I might warn you, too, that pulling your heartstrings from time to time isn't the only thing that'll happen in *Inspiration Point*. Why, at other points you'll get tickled and start laughing out loud, drawing strange looks from whoever happens to be sitting on the other side of the room! But it seems to me, if you have a tear in your eye one minute and you're laughing out loud the next, then you've been inspired.

And that's the goal of this little journey you've graciously agreed to take with me.

Okay, I guess I'd better back up. My conscience is starting to bother me a little. Maybe I wasn't being completely honest earlier when I said that I was kind of made of steel and immune—in Huck Finn's words—to sentimentality. Since we're going to be traveling together for awhile, I'd best go ahead and admit that sometimes as I read over some of my own stories, I get a little tear, too, and then a minute later—if I'm not really careful—I'll catch myself cracking up, just as you'll do. But please don't go spreading that around, if you don't mind, because I still have a couple hundred teenagers to teach every day and a good many basketball players to coach. I wouldn't want them to think I'm getting soft.

Regarding the title of the book, "Inspiration Point": I figure this is a place everybody has been to at one time or another and can't wait to go back. We've all visited a mountaintop and felt that inspiration as we looked out over the grandeur below.

I know that I feel that inspiration every time I stand on a high ledge somewhere in Tennessee looking out over the grand Smoky Mountains, or whenever I cross the Georgia line and see those tall pines imbedded deep in that Georgia red clay.

Some of you may have even been up on an "inspiration point" somewhere along the way with the love of your life, and you've looked out over a scene that was almost as grand as the joy you felt in your heart as you held the hand of that beautiful person. And your heart fluttered the whole time like little butterflies playing tag inside of you.

If you're thinking of that right now, *stop it!* That *isn't* what this book is about, and—I'll have to warn you—if you keep stopping along the way to pick flowers and listen to the creek whispering the way you're doing right now, this journey may take us a mighty long time. Come to think of it, that wouldn't be all bad, would it?

I will tell you, though, that this little journey does begin and end with a couple of stories of inspiration that take us to such an inspiring place, called Bromide Hill. I can't wait 'til we get there!

But we'll see many other "inspiration" points that we'll share as we walk together up this hill:

Riding along a dark road somewhere between Georgia and who knows where, listening to Preacher Miller tell a story. Ah, I'd like to go back there again.

Sitting by Mama's bedside reading from the Bible's greatest chapter.

Those are all trips to Inspiration Point.

There's Uncle Angus' giving me that special fifty-cent piece in 1973.

And my big brother Wayne standing in the vet's office doing the most courageous thing I've ever seen done.

And October 3.

Unforgettable inspiration points, the kind that shape a life for good.

There's a young fella named Jake running fifty yards for a touchdown, with fans from both sides hollering and cheering him on. I tried to take that story out, but all of my readers said, "No, you've gotta leave it in." Maybe you'll see why when you get to it.

Along the way, of course, there's also a brief visit with my dearest friend, the Man from Galilee, and I think you'll feel His presence in more than that one story.

Then there's sitting at Grandma's table. There's no place like that in the whole world. You'll understand what I'm about to tell you better as we walk along, but *Inspiration Point*, in many ways, is *her* story. I'll tell it to you every time we stop to rest, but I'll have to warn you that there'll probably be a little gleam in my eye and maybe more when we get to tip top of the Point. That's where I'll share the brilliant ending, as we look out together over those tall pines and Georgia red clay beneath. That's where it'll be okay to reach over and give me a little hug, because I might need one about then.

We'll share twenty-six stories in all (plus a bonus one at the end), mainly inspirational points several miles back in the rear-view mirror, but a few from just around the last curve.

So, my hiking friends, grab your tissue, tighten up your boot straps, pour yourself a cold glass of sweet tea, we're going for a little walk. It won't be long now 'til you'll find yourself up on a ledge looking out over one of those grand, august scenes that tend to take your breath away.

When you finally catch your breath, there won't be a doubt in your mind where you are.

Inspiration Point #1: Bromide Hill

In the little resort town of Sulphur, Oklahoma, a thousand people gather the week of July 4 for some of the best singing and preaching you'll find anywhere. But there's more that goes on in Sulphur than the singing and preaching. There's a special scene, high on a hill, that's almost as grand as those majestic songs and rafter-shaking sermons…

LOOKING LIFE OVER FROM BROMIDE HILL

A long time ago—way back in the '60s—Preacher Miller and Grandma began taking me to the little town of Sulphur, Oklahoma, for one of the most inspiring experiences I can remember…

We'd leave Georgia before the sun showed its face in the morning, head out west, and be in Sulphur, Oklahoma, before that sun turned in for the night.

For more than half a century, it has been the spot for church people to get together the week of July 4 to have the biggest gospel meeting of the year. Over a thousand people—from the orange groves of California all the way to the peach groves of Georgia—pull into this little town right about the first of July.

You'll hear more gospel singing and gospel preaching in a week than some folks will hear in a year.

For a whole week, Sulphur is a renovated town. It takes the town fifty-one weeks to recuperate from all the excitement. The sides are raised on the huge building we've always called the "tabernacle," located on several acres right in the middle of Sulphur. Older people who don't go to church sit out in their porch swings as the gospel hymns from a thousand tongues fill the night air and are carried on the cool breeze that accompanies the eventide.

If you listen really closely, you probably can hear the singing right now.

Then there's the preaching.

The preaching doesn't get any better than at Sulphur. The best preachers around pick out their best sermons. And being all fired up because of the nostalgia in the air and all the folks in the mile-long pews, they unleash the message with the vigor of a politician the day before election.

There are plenty of issues for the preachers to preach on, too, I can guarantee you that! I imagine I was one of 'em a time or two myself, back in my younger days—me and some of the fellas I ran around with, and me and a couple of girls I held hands with right there in the middle of the sermon. (I'd better set this straight: When I say a "couple" of girls, I don't mean at the same time, in case you're letting your imagination run away with you. If you were to believe some of the boys who knew me back then—which you shouldn't—they'd say I probably didn't hold hands with two girls *total* in all those years. But as we all know, fibbing is the first slippery step on the stairway of envy, as Mama used to tell me—or something like that.)

This brings me to the part about Sulphur I think you're going to like the best. Obviously, there's more going on at Sulphur than the singing and preaching, although those would be enough. Sulphur offers much more, though. The young man who is still a little wet behind the ears and finds himself slap in the middle of his dating years—well, he's the one who benefits the most.

You'll see.

After the night service, a mad scramble unlike anything you've ever seen will take place outside that grand old tabernacle. You'll see young fellas—not quite men, yet—running here and there, climbing or jumping a pew if it stands between them and a chance to converse with a lady all fixed up in a flowery dress and pretty ribbons in her hair. Why, it will get so spirited at times that a stranger passing by might think it was a holy-roller revival if he didn't see the church of Christ sign out front!

Now, I know about those boys jumping the pews and all, because I stood back and watched them do it. But that doesn't mean I was one *of* 'em. No sir, I never was caught doing that. For once in my life, I learned to do the smart thing. I'd get to the tabernacle early—all spruced up with my English Leather cologne and patent leather shoes—and watch as the girls arrived. Then about ten minutes before the singing and preaching would get started, I'd decide which one looked the prettiest. Then I'd go over to her and ask her if she'd like to go out later that night.

Now, I'll be the first—okay, maybe the last—to admit that it didn't always work out the way I hoped. One afternoon a bunch of us boys were playing a game of two-below football in a vacant lot by the tabernacle. Some of the girls, of course, came to watch. A girl named Teri caught my eye—I'll never forget that name, even though I've tried hard to—so right after I soared high to make a touchdown reception on an unbelievable one-handed grab in the corner of the end zone (this is my story, okay!?), I walked over, flipped the football in my hands skillfully, and said,

"Hey, Teri, would you like to go out tonight?"

I had asked that question many times with various results. But none of the previous results were even *close* to what she had in store for me. She looked at me a little funny, wrinkled her brow, and said:

"With whom?"

With that short question, she not only let me *have it*—as we say down South—but she let me have it with irritatingly perfect grammar! There's nothing worse than that!

I'll spare you the details of how the other fellas fell on the ground laughing their heads off when word got around the huddle about that. Suffice it to say it dampened the glory of that unbelievable, one-handed touchdown grab in the corner of the end zone.

But besides that little setback, I saw a distinct advantage of asking a girl out early. At least it gave you time to rebound should you ever get tackled in the backfield by a girl like Teri. The best part, though, is that by making your move early, you could get a lottery pick that night, maybe even the number one draft choice. Then the other guys would have to fight it out after the service over the rest of the girls still available in the first round. I've even known one or two who couldn't find a date until the second round or so. Your heart always went out to those boys.

There were other advantages to my system, too. I could sit by her through the two-hour service, and by the third song I'd be holding her hand and feeling mighty comfortable, seven or eight rows from the back. My buddies behind me would be shaking their heads and mumbling to themselves as they crossed out a name from their list.

Now, you may be wondering what a young fella and young lady'd do after hours in a little town like Sulphur. That's the good part. It's not so much what you do as what you feel.

You'll see what I mean.

Sulphur is a resort area, surrounded with mountains and streams and lakes and sightseeing trails and trees and waterfalls and...Bromide Hill. Bromide Hill overlooks the whole city and, I suppose, the surrounding cities as well, because—when you're standing up there looking out late at night—there are way too many lights just for Sulphur. I guess it is about the prettiest sight I ever remember. Up there on a warm, clear, July night, you could count the stars up above for the longest. And, if you ever got tired of that, you could watch the lights flicker down below.

Along the way, you and the young lady could lean against a rock and talk about things that seemed very important then and probably still should be. In between you might steal a kiss or two—that is, if you knew how to work it. If not, you might end up finding Mars and Jupiter and then counting every star in the Milky Way and the Big Dipper, and the Little Dipper, too. That's something that happened to all of us boys one time or another, I guess, although I never heard any of them admit it.

After a couple of years, the fellas I tackled and blitzed during the day and *really* competed with at night kind of outgrew Bromide Hill.

But I never did.

I pretended to, but I never outgrew that place.

Still to this day, there's hardly a place like Bromide Hill in the whole world. I still go back there about once a year, and more than that if you count the times I look up at the stars on a clear night, no matter where I am.

July 1996

The rest of the story

One more thing, while we sit on this little rock and rest a minute:

I need to tell you the rest of the story. I mentioned that a young man in his dating years would likely be the one to benefit the most from the Sulphur experience. But of all the boys who benefited, *I* came out better than them all, even despite a few heartbreaks along the way.

It was at Sulphur that I met a little blonde who knew what I was talking about when I said, "Would you like to go out?"

And she would become my amazing wife.

Later that little blonde would give me a son with a great personality—Mal—and a terrific third-grade-teaching daughter, Rachel.

Then, on February 9, 2005, Rachel gave me one of the most inspirational gifts I've ever received: a little grandson named Connor Reed, better known to my readers as Little Dewey.

All of that because Preacher Miller and Grandma took me to Sulphur, Oklahoma, where I learned to hold hands while a thousand voices sang "How Beautiful Heaven Must Be."

One day we'll have to make a return trip to Inspiration Point, because you'll want to hear about this little Dewey and his knack for inspiration. But to give you a little preview, I'll include one of his stories in a little bonus section at the end before we head back down the mountain.

But for now, I'd like to take you to another inspiration point, this one involving a big brother's most courageous moment.

Inspiration Point #2:

My big brother Wayne taught me to love basketball, our dog Chico, and the Yankees. He even
took time out one day and tried to teach me
about the birds and the bees. But that was about
a week after he told me a big one about there not
being a Santa Claus, so—after that—I wasn't
about to believe anything he said.

But some lessons you learn whether you want to
or not, and that happened one heart-wrenching
day in a doctor's office in 1968. What I learned
that day made the lessons at West Side Junior
High seem easier than watching Saturday morning cartoons…

BIG BROTHER TAUGHT THE TRUE MEANING OF COURAGE

Being the baby in the family, I depended on my big brothers to teach me a good bit about life…

Wayne was nearer my age than Tim, so the lot fell on him a little more to show me around.

And he did.

He taught me to love the Yankees, although I chose Roger Maris as my hero while he opted for Mickey Mantle.

He taught me to love basketball, too, and laughed when I was too little to get the ball to the rim.

He even tried to tell me about the birds and the bees one day in 1968 while I was mopping the kitchen floor. Obviously, that didn't go over too well.

Maybe the most important thing he taught me was the meaning of courage, something I still haven't forgotten.

Wayne and I grew up with a little dog named Chico. I must have only been three or four years old when we went across town and picked out the mutt. He was the runt, and he looked the part. He was white—kind of a dingy white—and was part Chihuahua and part I don't know what all. He probably wouldn't have brought seventy-five cents on the street.

But Chico—named after La Grange High football star and later my coach and teacher, Chico Lynch—was a big part of our family, as dogs tend to be. He was always a step or two behind either Wayne or me as we strolled down from Juniper Street to Truitt Avenue to play with our Bailey cousins or to visit Grandma's. Or he'd lead the way down seven or eight hills as we bounced our way to the Y to play basketball.

Chico even had a knack for going to church. He followed us there a hundred times when we'd walk the three or four blocks to the church on the corner of Murphy and Fourth. It didn't take him long to figure out where we were going when we got dressed up and started walking up the hill or got in the car on a Sunday or Wednesday. By the time they let church out, we'd find him outside waiting for us patiently, and he'd always greet us with that dingy white tail just a-wagging.

I hate to say it, but there for a while he got to going to church better than some of our regular members. And he never let a headache keep him home or complained about having to get dressed to go.

Ah, Chico was quite a dog.

He was the first dog I ever saw get chased by a cat. He got after a cat one day when we were over on Truitt at Grandma's. The cat ran from Chico for a while, then he must have got to thinking that Chico didn't look all that tough. So he turned around and started chasing Chico. Chico may not have been a thoroughbred, but he was a quick thinker, and he knew he didn't want to go toe to claw with a mean cat. When he saw that cat coming at him, he pulled the emergency brake, yanked it into first gear, and started burning rubber.

Fortunately for Chico, cats don't have an instinct for chasing dogs, so the cat gave up even before Chico figured out he wasn't going to be able to get up that chinaberry tree in Grandma's yard.

Chico didn't actually get up the tree when the cat got after him. But it wasn't for a lack of trying!

I know being chased by a cat embarrassed Chico, because when the cat went on its way, Chico lowered his head and walked on home by himself and didn't bother to wait to run home with Wayne or me.

Chico stayed around with us all through the growing up years and was as much a part of the family as anybody. But when I was about twelve, he developed some bad health. He'd certainly had a good life, having chased—if my calculations are correct—10, 950 squirrels in his life-time, without catching one. That's bound to be some kind of record. (By the way, that's three squirrels a day for ten years, and I'm guessing that number's on the low side.)

Even though Chico had had a good life, I still wasn't nearly ready to give him up. You never are.

Wayne figured out before I did that Chico's squirrel-chasing and church-going days were over. Chico started swelling up badly, and a few times he'd be walking around the house and would just fall over. Each time we thought he was a goner, but he got up off the mat each time and was able to fight a few more rounds. Finally, Mama told Wayne and me we'd better take him to the vet. I didn't like the sound of her voice when she said it.

So we put Chico in Wayne's big, green '59 Buick and hauled him to the doc.

Something else I didn't like was the way Chico acted when Doc checked him over. He just lay there not saying a word. He didn't even complain when Doc poked on him, so I knew he was pretty bad.

But being pretty bad didn't mean I was even close to giving up hope.

Finally the doc looked at Wayne and me and said there wasn't anything he could do for Chico, that he really was suffering a lot. He said we could take him home or we could let him put him to sleep.

I knew what I wanted to do. That was a no-brainer. I came *this close* to shouting out loud: "Doc, we'll take him home! He'll be okay in a few days. You watch and see!"

Wayne didn't say anything for a minute.

Again I started to help my big brother out and grab Chico and say, "Let's go," but I couldn't get the words to come out. Instead I just watched him mull over a decision that was as easy as choosing ice cream over spinach.

We put Chico in Wayne's big, green '59 Buick and hauled him to the doc.

Finally he said, "Doc, do what you gotta do."

Wayne and I didn't talk on the way home, and I don't know that we've ever discussed that day since. My big sister Jean said that when we walked in the house and Wayne had Chico's collar in his hand, she and Mama knew. Nobody had to say a word.

I didn't appreciate Wayne too much that day, nor the next few teary-eyed days, either. But as the years have come and gone, I've figured out that Wayne taught me a pretty important lesson.

I still think it was the most courageous thing I've ever seen anybody do.

November 1999

Inspiration Point #3:

Take a deep breath, because we've come to a point where I need to share one of the most touching memories I keep folded away in my mind. It's a memory of Mama, nearing her final mile, listening as I read the Bible with a trembly voice in August of 1973. When she held up her hand and stopped me in the middle of one of the Bible's sweetest passages, she asked me a question I've spent the last thirty years trying to answer. If you don't mind, I might have to ask you to look out yonder over the tall pines while I tell this one…

MAMA'S CHALLENGE!

Challenges are bigger when they come from Mama.

At least the last one Mama ever gave me was.

I think about it every time I take a deep, hard look inside.

I guess I always will.

As I think of Mama now, it's hard for me to believe that I've now lived longer than she did, or that in a couple of days she'll have been gone for a quarter of a century.

She was a remarkable woman, Mama, made from a rare and precious cloth. I think if she had lived during Bible times, the Lord would have pointed her out in a crowd and said, "I've not seen such faith, no, not in all of Israel." That's the kind of Christian woman she was. She worked hard all her life—most of it down at Callaway's cotton mill—working to support three boys and a girl by herself because Daddy had health problems most of their married lives, before he died in '67.

I don't think I ever went in that cotton mill, although I've passed by it a thousand times. But I can imagine the difficulty of a lady spinning her life along in a hot mill. For Mama, it was a small thing. I never heard her complain, nor was she envious of others who had much more and worked much less. I know that the beans and cornbread and stew she put on the table each night after a full day's work was more than enough for the four of us.

I always thought we were kind of rich. We had everything we needed. I didn't realize until I was grown that we were pretty much poor folks, Mama never making more than about $1.60 an hour in all those years of working. It's amazing how a poor lady could build a house of gold on those kinds of wages.

Mama took care of her family, everything from a runny nose to a cavity on a bottom left molar. About once a year, Mama would drive us up to Griffin where this old dentist would give us a little "gas" and then go to town on a bad tooth with a high-powered drill of his that felt more like a jackhammer to me than a drill. The gas, I remember, helped, though. It made me feel I was only *dreaming* somebody was trying to drill a hole through my jaw instead of it actually happening. I never liked that trip, but Mama—in her own words—wasn't about to let "the teeth rot out of your head, not as long as I'm your mama."

Of the four children, I was the youngest. But that's not how Mama said it. Whenever we'd meet somebody she knew who had never met me, she'd say (with her face glowing with pride), "And this is my *baby*." That made me mad. Nothing ever made me any madder than that did.

As soon as we were alone, I'd say, "Mama, why do you have to do that? I'm not a baby. I'm ten and a half going on 11. I'm almost a man."

And Mama would just smile without ever saying a word.

I sure wish Mama was here today, because I'd let her call me her "baby" all she wanted. Unfortunately, her time was shortened and she never saw that baby become a man.

But she came close.

In her latter days, with a brain tumor issuing her both blind and lame at the young age of 42 (my own age now), she'd have me come to her bedside at Grandma's house to read the Bible to her. Grandma took care of Mama for the last few months of her life, kind of the way she took care of her sweet daughter when she was a baby. It's one of the things I most appreciate about my grandma.

The Lord preserved Mama's most valuable sense— her mind—and she loved most of all to hear the reading of the Bible. Not long before her death (I remember it clearly)—on a night in early August, 1973, the day before my 17th birthday—she asked me to sit by the bed and read to her.

There didn't seem to be any place to turn and read except Paul's chapter of love—the thirteenth chapter of First Corinthians. With what must have been a quivering voice, I read the story of Mama's life right there in the words of the great apostle. I read the life of a lady who worked in a cotton mill and came home to make stew and beans and hauled us to the Lord's house three times or more a week and to the dentist fifty miles away once a year.

I came to that portion of the scripture at the end of the chapter of love where the great apostle writes,

"When I was child, I spoke as a child, I understood as a child, I thought as a child. But when I became a man, I put away childish things."

Mama gathered her strength—ah, I'll never forget this—lifted her hand for me to pause, and turned her dimmed eyes toward me. I took her hand and waited to see what she had to say. The words she spoke rang out louder than any I'd ever heard, and they have carried me now through a quarter of a century.

There didn't seem to be any place to turn and read except Paul's chapter of love—the thirteenth chapter of First Corinthians.

"Son," Mama said, "Are *you* goin' to become a man tomorrow?"

I could offer my dear lady in return nothing more than a faint and graspy assurance that I would. It took a good while for me to gather myself to finish reading—through blurred vision—the story of love. I sat there for some time holding her hand that night, as she faded off to sleep and as I tried to understand what she had said and what she expected of me.

As I think of Mama now—twenty-five years later—I

realize that it wasn't so hard for that baby of hers to become a man. The weaving and spinning of a quarter of a century takes care of most of that task for you. The harder task is trying to become like Mama. I've found *that* to be a job a mere twenty-five years can't handle. It's a job of a lifetime.

October 1998

Inspiration Point #4

Life gets complicated as we try to make our way in the world, chasing dreams that can be as slippery as some of our childhood buddies in a game of tag. But there's one place where life stays simple, and I've found it important to return there whenever I can…But I have to warn you: When we get to Grandma's house, you'd better be ready to stay for a while. We'll have to leave eventually. But when we do, a different person will walk out her back door than the one who walked in. Grandma will do that to you…

WHAT'LL IT BE: COLLARD, MUSTARD, OR TURNIP GREENS, TONIGHT?

Do you know of anything that compares to being at Grandma's?…

I don't, and I've been gone from my Georgia home for a quarter of a century, ever since Mama ended her walk in 1973.

I was reminded of how it feels to be at Grandma's on my most recent trip back home. I hadn't been out of the car a minute before I knew that I was back home in the deep South.

No, it wasn't the kudzu on the side of the road or the tall pines or the red clay, although those are some definite signs. But I knew I was back home when I walked into that humble little house where lives an eighty-eight year old lady who always treats me like a king from the minute I walk in the door until I pack up and head back west.

I arrived at Grandma's on a Friday evening, and when I walked in, she gave me the evening's menu almost before she gave me a hug.

"What'd you want tonight for supper?" she asked. "I've got collard greens, turnip greens, or mustard greens."

I couldn't help but to smile because I knew where I was.

No place but home.

Nowhere but the South.

Nobody but Grandma.

For the better part of a week I enjoyed the simple pleasures of being home with Grandma. For breakfast it was eggs and grits and hot homemade biscuits with sorghum syrup and crisp bacon and coffee (cream and sugar, of course) and orange juice.

Every morning.

That's the gospel truth.

Grandma is always in the kitchen waiting to put the eggs and biscuits on as soon as I wake up. There's no alarm clock, either. For a rare few days in the year, my body gets up when it's good and ready to get up, not a moment sooner, better not mess with it.

Then, in the evening, it's hot cornbread with home-grown green beans, fresh corn, onion, and whatever the "greens" of the day is, all topped off with a glass of butter-milk and cornbread (the latter is always my personal choice, and I'd sure recommend it to anybody who'd like to try it). On some visits there's even a saucer with fried green tomatoes or fried apple pies.

After each meal we sit and talk. Then I clean off the table while she washes the dishes. She doesn't let me wash dishes. I may be the king, but she's still the boss. I run around during the day, but we always gather together again at night, when I sit and write and she sits and reads the Bible. Along the way we always stop to talk about some great Bible story, the way we recently talked about the friendship of David and Jonathan over there in the book of First Samuel.

You may find all of this a little simplistic. I know I do. There's something about coming home and breaking life down to its most simple elements, before heading back west and tackling a hundred challenges that await me the minute the plane hits the runway.

It just seems to me that there's something really healthy about breaking life down to those most simple elements, just like it's healthy to sit at a table with mustard, turnip, or collard greens.

But, for me, the healthiest part of all is sitting at the table with Grandma.

April 1998

Inspiration Point #5:

Preacher Miller was a man who stood head and shoulders above the rest. He could really preach it with his raspy booming voice, even making the rafters shake and rattle when he got on a roll. When he was done with a sermon, he knew how to close the deal. He closed many of 'em on a cold night down at an icy river or lake. Of all the folks he baptized through the years—and there must have been a thousand—the one I most remember is a young boy in June 1967…

THE MAN WHO WET HIS PANTS NIGHT AFTER NIGHT

Elbert Harvey Miller was a giant of a man…

Growing up, there were more than a few giants in my life, folks who were just a little bigger than life. But none stands taller than Preacher Miller.

This legendary Southern fellow brushed my path almost every day for the first seventeen years of my life. To come to think of it, he still brushes my path every day, even now, although he's been gone for eight years. That's how big a fella he was.

This man was a pioneer, old-timey, backwoods, tell-it-like-it-is, Bible-quoting, church of Christ preacher. Obviously, he was not your run of the mill, ordinary preacher, not by a long shot. When you'd look at him standing up in that pulpit, he looked seven feet tall, especially if you hadn't hit double digits in years yet. And even if you were quite a bit more than that, you still had to admit he preached that tall, if nothing else.

He didn't know much about today's modern psychology and philosophy. He just preached an old-fashioned gospel that would do one of two things: It'd either save you or it'd convict you.

There wasn't any middle ground.

After he raised the roof and shook the rafters for an hour—not necessarily in that order—you wouldn't be walking out of there riding the fence. He'd make you take your stand on the right hand or on the left—preferably on the right, but you could choose the left if you wanted.

During his preaching days covering more than half a century—most of it right here in my Georgia hometown, although he spent quite a bit of time traveling the country preaching, too—more than a thousand folks, I guess, would come in on the left hand. But before the singing and praying and preaching were over, they'd go out on the right hand. He'd take them out to an old creek or a running river or a cow tank and baptize them while the crowd coming to watch would sing "O Happy Day" with enough vigor that the animals in the woods would gather around to see what was going on. At least, that's what they'd tell me. I never did actually see it myself, but it wouldn't have surprised me if I had.

More than once he had to break the ice on the river before immersing a convert, but—because I think he had ice water in his veins when it came time to preach or baptize—I don't think he knew the water was cold.

Sometimes at the end of a sermon, he'd notify the congregation in his loud, raspy voice that always caught their attention: "Awright, brothers, sisters, and friends, tomorrow night I plan on *wettin' my pants!*" And, usually, he'd have them wringing wet by the next night, and two or three other people's too—down at the river!

He'd notify the congregation in his loud, raspy voice:
"Tomorrow night I plan on wettin' my pants!"

That's how Preacher Miller became known as the man
who wet his pants night after night.

Of all his baptisms, the one I remember most was that
of a young ten-year-old boy in June of 1967. This young
fella walked up when they sang the invitation song, took
Preacher Miller's big hand, and told him he wanted to be
baptized.

After Preacher Miller had told the story of the eunuch
of Acts chapter eight, and after he had asked the young boy
to make that grand confession—"I believe Jesus Christ is
the son of God"—Preacher Miller took the nervous young
lad back to the baptistery, took his hand, walked him down
into the water, raised that giant arm of his, and declared
that he was baptizing him in the name of Jesus Christ for

the remission of sins, into the name of the Father, Son, and Holy Spirit.

Then the preacher-man lowered him down into the water to fulfill the young fella's most glorious hour.

That young boy came drenching wet out of the water with Mama and Daddy and Grandma and brothers and sisters and friends of a lifetime looking on proudly.

I've never been the same since.

October 4, 1997

One more thing as we pause to rest…

I wrote this story of the great preacher on October 4, 1997. It seems appropriate that six years later, on October 4, 2003, Preacher Miller's lifelong helpmeet—and my Grandma—would take her greatest journey. We'll need to move on up the mountain for now, but in a little while—when we get to the Point—we'll sit together and rehearse that story. I'll be looking forward to that.

Inspiration Point #6

As it is with most best friends, it's hard to remember exactly when I first met this one. I've known Him far longer than I can remember. Mama and Preacher Miller and Grandma made sure of that. I love telling stories, but His story is the one I love to tell the most…

I STILL LOVE TO TELL THE STORY

Friends are pretty near the best things around, and there's never been one better than the Man from Galilee …

His story is the greatest I've ever told and the one, even today, I love the most.

There is none to compare.

To tell it in a page or two is impossible, but I can at least introduce Him to you, just as Preacher Miller and Grandma and Mama and many others introduced Him to me a long time ago.

One of the reasons I like to see a year wind down is that it is during those wintry days of December that the world focuses on Jesus the Christ more than any other time of the year. The scenes and songs that fill the air are heart-warming, and the story of the babe born in a manger is inspiring.

But there's more to the story, and I like to tell it all.

Years ago—when I was a young boy of almost eleven who had recently gone down into the water with Preacher Miller—I was asked to step up and lead a song at the old, red brick church of Christ building in my southern hometown. I'll always remember the title of the hymn. After thirty-plus years, in a way it kind of tells my own life story:

"I love to tell the story."

And I do. I still do. I think I love to tell it more now than ever. It means more. I've had more years to weigh its value. I have the burden of plenty of failures, too, that give the story and its message more meaning.

It is still the story of a beautiful child born in Bethlehem, born among the animals in a barn.

But it's more.

It's the story of a Man who ate with sinners and healed the diseases of the afflicted and gave strength to the weary and hope to the discouraged.

It's the story of more than a man—the son of God—who would take men whose lives were battered and torn, and He'd mold them so that when they walked away you wouldn't recognize who they were at all.

It's the story of the King of kings finishing supper, then tossing a towel over His shoulder and taking a basin of water and bowing down to wash the feet of his disciples. This is one of my favorite scenes of all, because it reminds me that there are plenty of feet around that I could be washing. It reminds me to strive to be a servant, not a king.

It's the story of a Man who—when He washed the disciples' feet—washed the feet of a man by the name of Judas.

This story is of a Man who happened upon the scene where a lady stood facing a mob with rocks in their hands, ready to condemn her for her sins. When the Lord had finished reading the stories of those men's lives, they walked away in shame, and the lady—because of the Man from Galilee—walked away with redeeming grace in her hands.

I love to tell the story of the blind man who had never

seen a single thing his whole life.

Until he met Jesus.

That evening, this blind man stood and watched for the first time as the sun went down, scattering and blending its colors of orange and blue and yellow and gray throughout the western horizon. Then—as John records in the ninth chapter of that gospel—he cried out the words of another great hymn, "I was blind, but now I see."

It's a story of a master Storyteller, standing before the multitudes and telling of the boy who ran away from home but later retraced his steps back to his father's house with nothing but rags on his back and an apology on his lips.

But there's more to this story, much more than a page can hold.

It's a story of a Man who carried a cross up a hill called Calvary, a story of a man with nail scars in His hands.

But the biography of Jesus doesn't end that dark day outside Jerusalem.

Triumphantly, there's an empty tomb and a risen Saviour and a reigning King.

That's the story I like to tell.

So, now, thirty years after my first feeble attempt to stand and lead a song among my congregation of friends, I still carry a song with me, as though it were just yesterday.

And I carry its message:

"I love to tell the story, more wonderful it seems, than all the golden glories, than all our golden dreams..."

Ah, I love to tell it, even as I've told it just now.

December 22, 2001

Inspiration Point #7

Uncle Angus had many distinguishing trademarks. He could take his teeth out and touch his nose to his chin. He could take the longest time of anybody I ever knew in answering a question. And he could give a gift that would stay with a young Georgia boy even when he was scraping the bottom of the barrel…

UNCLE ANGUS AND THE FIFTY-CENT PIECE

Georgia never had a native son with more unique trademarks than Uncle Angus…

I still can't help but smile when I think of some of them and the mark they left on me. But the one mark he made way back in 1973 still makes me shake my head the most.

First I should tell you that Uncle Angus wasn't my "real" uncle. He was the uncle of my best friend Coca-Cola Mike I grew up with down the Georgia way. But I always called him my uncle right alongside Coca-Cola. He was as much an uncle as one could be.

Coca-Cola and I spent a good many childhood days laughing at Uncle Angus' ways. He could clean his plate with a piece of cornbread at the end of a meal better than anybody I've ever seen. His plate would be cleaner at the end of a meal than it was at the beginning.

And he could take his false teeth out and touch his chin to his nose. I went years before seeing that again, and never would have, I don't think, if Coca-Cola Mike and his family hadn't gone down to Gatlinburg, Tennessee, one year on vacation and brought back a video of a man who looked a lot like Uncle Angus doing the same trick himself in a comedy routine. Like Uncle Angus, he had that long, pointed nose and quarter-of-a-moon-shaped chin that it took to get those two body parts to meet.

Maybe Uncle Angus' most notable trademark was his way of answering a question. You'd ask him something, and he'd chew on it the longest time, as if the question was a piece of tough meat. After a minute or two—just when you thought he didn't hear the question—he'd spit out the answer in a profound way.

Uncle Angus always called his wife "Bounce." Coca-Cola and I asked him why he did that one evening while he was out back snapping string beans. He churned it over in his mind a while, but pretty soon the sun starting going down. We figured he had forgotten the answer—or maybe the question—so we started heading to the house. But about the time we got to the gate of his fence we heard him grunt, so we turned back:

"'Cause she bounces!" he said.

Then he went about his business, paying us no mind.

We wanted to ask him what that meant, but we figured there wasn't nearly enough daylight left for that, so we let it rest.

Those kinds of puzzling responses by Uncle Angus were probably the reason Bounce was always finding fault with him. She was a handful for him to handle, to be sure. She was taller than he was (and a little meaner, too, I think), so he had to be careful how he handled things around her.

One day they were in the garden picking beans, but, as usual, he had her doing all the work. He was just ordering her around, the way he liked to do.

"Quit orderin' me around, Angus," she said. "You just

want to oversee me. That's all you want to do."

"Hm," Uncle Angus said, not cracking a smile, "I can't do that. You're way too tall. It'd take a six-foot ladder to oversee you."

Then he let out one of those laughs that sounded as if he were hyperventilating, and dodged as she threw a stringed bean at him.

Ah, I think I'll always remember Uncle Angus for those special trademarks. But the most permanent mark he left on me was something he did when I was seventeen, on a cool October night in 1973, the day before I was to leave those Georgia roots and head to Texas. Outside the church where we had worshipped together all of my life, Uncle Angus came up to me and gave me a Kennedy half dollar that Sunday night.

"If you don't spend this, you'll never be broke," he said, and—as I think back to it—I believe he said it the same way he had said, "'Cause she bounces."

I can see him standing there as if it were yesterday. I knew I didn't have time to ask what that meant, so I took the half dollar without thinking too much about it or what he said, and took off to Texas, where I would have to make my way in the world. I kept that fifty-cent piece and never spent it. As the years passed, he slowly answered the question I never asked.

That fifty-cent piece became a link to a past, to that good ol' Georgia red clay, to a heritage. As long as I held onto that, and as long as I remembered what he said, I would remember where I came from and what I was taught while I was there. The more I think about it, the more I realize that that simple gift has played a part in helping me face the world these past thirty years.

And while I must admit I've sometimes scraped the bottom of the barrel since 1973, thanks to the man who could touch his chin to his nose and could take all day to answer a question, I've never been broke!

June 1996

(adapted from *That Southern Red Clay Jus' won't Wash Off*)

Let's pause here at this rock just for a moment...

You've probably noticed as we've walked and talked that the stories and the lives of the people we're sharing seem to touch one another's. They kind of merge.

This is certainly true of Uncle Angus.

He and Preacher Miller served together as elders at the church of Christ at Murphy and Fourth Avenue in La Grange for many years, at least twenty or thirty.

Uncle Angus and "Bounce," along with Preacher Miller and Grandma, also shared a tragic moment in their lives. They were driving home from a gospel meeting in Marietta, Georgia, late one summer night in the 60s when they were hit head-on by a car drag racing in the wrong lane of that two-lane highway.

The boys in the racing car didn't survive, but the Lord was with my four loved ones.

Bounce received minor scrapes, nothing more, as I remember. Grandma and Uncle Angus received some pretty serious facial injuries, and I can remember Grandma's face being black and blue all over. I learned recently that Uncle Angus broke about every bone in his face in the accident—including his nose—which might explain his special gift of bringing that long nose and that long chin together when his teeth were being soaked—or any other time he wanted to plop his teeth out without notice.

Preacher Miller, who was driving, was the most seriously injured one, shattering his hip. It was bad enough that the doctor told him he would never walk again.

But Preacher Miller said,

"Ah, Doc, you and me and the Lord can do better than that!"

Sure enough, in six weeks he was walking with crutches and back in the pulpit preaching on a walker not long after that. He had a little hitch in his step from that day on, but that didn't keep him from walking many a mile after that.

I remember, too, that Uncle Angus touched the life of Mama in a special way. This is the account I had in mind to tell you when we first stopped to lean on the rock.

A good many years after I left Georgia and moved to Texas, I visited Uncle Angus in his huge, 100-year-old or more home next door to my childhood home on Juniper Street. I say "next door," and it was, but there was a road—or paved hill—that separated our two homes.

As we visited that evening out on his screened-in back porch, Uncle Angus pointed out an azalea that grew near the road in our yard. Of course, it wasn't "our" yard anymore, because we had sold the house a good while back. But it is still ours in one way and will always be.

Uncle Angus looked out over our yard, and said, "Steve, see that azalea with all those blooms over by the road?"

"Yes sir," I said.

"I gave that to your mama a long time ago, back when you were little-bitty. I bought three of those azaleas and gave them all away. Your mama planted that one out there. I think you helped her do it. And it's lived all this time. But the other two I gave away didn't live a week."

I appreciated that little story, because whenever I'm back home, I love remembering all the good things. It makes me feel good down deep inside. You understand. I guess that's what *Inspiration Point* is all about, really. I hope you're remembering your own points of inspiration as we're walking along, and I hope they give you that good down-deep feeling, too.

Uncle Angus touched a great number of lives—not just mine, but the lives of those closest to me. In addition to that fifty-cent piece he gave me in the church yard that Sunday evening, he gave me that other special gift that day on his back porch.

He reminded me of Mama's special touch.

I think he did it on purpose.

Inspiration Point #8

Chase Freeman has had a hard life, in jail more than he's been out during his adult life. But there's one moment in his life that stands out, at least in my book. Down at Mud Creek one summer day in 1965, he dived in the water to do his most heroic deed. I'm mighty glad he did…

CHASE FREEMAN A MUD CREEK HERO

Heroes can be right around the corner, and you not even know it...

So it was with Chase Freeman, my soft-spoken, humble, easy-going cousin whose only flaw is that he sometimes ends up on the wrong side of the law.

I don't know what made me think of this story all of a sudden, but when it came to mind I remembered why I like Chase so much.

You'll understand later.

As kids, we always went swimming off of a little dirt road off of the Whitesville Road at a waterhole called Mud Creek. I don't know how we came upon this little swimming hole five or six miles out of town, unless it was because my grandparents on my daddy's side used to own some land a couple of miles down from Mud Creek.

But one summer day—probably around 1965—a bunch of us cousins went swimming out at the creek. Chase's Uncle Gene, who was about twenty at the time, loaded us in his car and hauled us out there.

I don't know if Mud Creek still carries the same name

as it did then or if it was its official name at all. It may just have been what we called it. But it wore its name well. It was nothing but a muddy ol' creek flowing under a bridge way out on a road that didn't lead to anywhere in particular. I guess Mud Creek's distinction was that it did carry quite a bit of water between its banks, especially in that little spot we had found under that bridge. Unlike most creeks, this one had water as deep as five or six feet in spots, maybe more, and at times its current flowed along pretty speedily, too.

There's another distinction about Mud Creek: I learned to swim there. It seemed to be fifteen yards from one side of the creek to the other, although if I went back now I think I'd find that it wasn't any more than fifteen feet. But somewhere in my growing up years, I learned to dog paddle from one side of that creek to the other in water that was significantly higher than my four-foot frame. I was still a few years away from hitting double digits when I got skilled at the art of dog paddling. Since that was a few years before the more sophisticated Pine Lake came onto the scene, Mud Creek was our only swimming teacher.

On this summer day, we boys had been swimming for a while when Gene told us to get ready to go, that he was going up on the bridge for a smoke. We weren't quite ready to go, because the water was deep and the current swift due to a good rain that had come the night before. We were having too much fun to follow orders the first time, so we ignored them and kept on splashing and diving along. After a couple of smokes, Gene hollered down again—this time with a tone I think he got from his Navy experience—and said his beat-up blue car was leaving in two minutes, with or without us.

All the boys shrugged and mumbled but obeyed and

starting climbing out of the water, along with me. But once I got to the bank, I thought I would take one last dive before getting out for good.

Just one final little-bitty one for the road.

So I took my dive. The next thing I remember is being stuck in the middle of that creek with the current running over my head. I was dog paddling like crazy but not moving an inch. I was hung there, just fighting the water. I still remember the images well. All I could see were yellow water and bubbles. The image stayed the same. It was even a little peaceful. I don't remember being particularly scared, although I did get choked up some on the way home.

Being stuck just beneath the surface of that sun-aided yellow water is all that I know to tell you. I have to depend on the other boys' eyewitness accounts for the rest of the details. They said that all you could see was my hair sticking out of the water. Chase, they said, saw me first and dived in to get me. Then Gene, when he heard all the carrying on below, came running and descended that steep, sand-bagged embankment in two giant steps and followed Chase head first.

I vaguely remember them pulling me out of the water. But I distinctly remember everyone talking about how it was Chase that saved me. Gene came at the end to make sure the job was done right, but Chase was the hero. He'd seen me in the water, and, at only four years older, put his own eleven-year-old life on the line to save me.

Chase, they said, saw me first and dived in to get me.

Now, after four decades, I don't know how many good things Chase has done to add to his list. It may be a pretty short list. Probably is. But even though my own list sure isn't as long as it should be, the way I figure it, anything I have on my list can go on his, too. After all, if not for Chase, I wouldn't even *have* a list. You know what I mean.

I wanted to tell you that story now so you'd know why Chase is a hero of mine. I never got around to thanking him for that, I guess, and I don't know his current address exactly. So I hope some of my kin folks will share this story with him as my way of saying thanks—that is, until I can do it myself.

It's going to surprise ol' Chase when he reads this, because he may have probably forgotten the whole thing. I hope not, because it's one of the best things he's done his whole life.

At least, I think it was.

June 23, 2001

Let's catch our breath again, just for a minute…

You'll be glad to know that Chase has gotten himself on the right track now and is out of jail and back in church. That's a pretty good one-two punch, I think. I can't wait to get back home and see him. It's been a long time.

I hadn't seen Gene in many years, either, until October of 2003. (You'll find out later why I saw him back in Georgia at that time.) When we visited, Gene and I laughed about the Mud Creek incident, and he tried to straighten me out on some of the details. The whole thing was cemented in my mind too firmly for me to make any significant changes, though.

But I was glad he remembered, even if his memory was slipping some.

This past spring—2006—news from down South came that Gene had died suddenly of a heart attack. That was a pretty big shock, because he was only in his late 50s. It made me re-think the story of Mud Creek, and it made me remember how many people his life had touched, too.

Gene was about the same age as my sister Jean. Growing up they ran around together with a redheaded lady named Louise Fling, all of whom attended the church there at Fourth and Murphy. I won't be able to tell you all of Louise's story here—maybe we'll do that on a future trip to Inspiration Point—but I want to show you again how lives intertwine.

I had a chance to visit Louise a year ago, because she had been diagnosed with cancer a few months earlier. In our visit, she showed me her sea shell collection, and I wrote a couple of columns about her and those sea shells in the *La Grange Daily News.* She also showed me something on her refrigerator that I thought was amazing.

It was a list of "good people," I think she called it. There were pictures and newspaper clippings about many people who had touched her life through the years. One of her good people was my Grandma. They weren't kin, but Grandma touched many more lives than just that of a young, nostalgic grandson.

I thought it was interesting that she also had a picture of Gene on her refrigerator. I don't know why, exactly, but I know he touched her life. He had to've. He made her list of good people.

Gene touched mine, too, I can tell you that! You don't help pull somebody out of the water without making a lasting impression.

Of course, Chase Freeman is the charter member of that club.

I guess I have a good many heroes, like Gene, Chase, and Louise. Of those three, only Chase still walks that Georgia red clay.

But the further we hike up Inspiration Point, the more often we're reminded that people who inspire you along the way keep inspiring you, regardless.

Our "October 3" story is next, and we'll see it again.

It's time to share that story, so we'd better get back on the trail.

Inspiration Point #9

October 3 is a special day—a sad day, in a way, but very special in another. On this day the good Lord took something very important away, and it would take Him almost twenty years to pay it back. But when He did, He did it fourfold…

BLESSINGS COME IN PACKAGES OF FOUR

I pause to count my blessings each year as the third of October rolls around…

You might think it strange that I would say that, since on this day in 1973 my mama, Fanny Louise Bowen, ended her journey.

But, amazingly—in spite of that—I count October 3 as a special day.

We learn, after a while, to thank the good Lord for what He gives us, not for what He has to take away. And I know God gave me something special when He gave me Mama.

It's not just me who thinks so, either. Occasionally—when I'm back home or when some friend of Mama's writes me after reading a column in the *La Grange Daily News*—I'll get a tribute to her from somebody who worked with her in the cotton mill or knew her otherwise. Without fail, they tell me how sweet and wonderful the good lady was. Through all my years, I've never heard anybody say otherwise.

I guess they know better.

You can understand why I might stop—even on that memorable day in October—and count the blessings of having had such a remarkable lady touch my life. And it's true: That's one of the big blessings I count on October 3 every year.

But I count my blessings for a different reason, too. You see, on the third day of October—eighteen years after Mama walked the last mile of her way—the Lord showered down some amazing blessings. If it could be done, He out-did even Himself this time. Four little ones, born together, introduced themselves to the world.

And to my life and to the life of my family.

October 3, 1991.

These four blonde-headed babies, quadruplets, are four of our best friends today.

So, on their ninth birthday…I grabbed my bag of presents and headed over to make my delivery to my four best friends.

Austin, Grant, Lexi, and Candice.

Friends of mine.

They were born to a mom and dad I grew up with, two people who have been gracious enough to let me and my family adopt their four babies as kind of our own.

You've gotta meet 'em.

First there's Candice. She's the one who's always thriving on attention, always clinging, hanging on you 'til you collapse. Sometimes that may be a little too much to some people.

But not for me.

I've been around long enough to know that great nine-year-old friends are hard to come by. Candice knows it, too. She knows that if she ever needs to cling to somebody, I'm the fella. Young Candice, don't ever forget that.

Then there's Grant.

I call him Grant-man.

The cute one.

The one with the quick wit.

The one most likely to be quoted.

The one most likely to spend time in "time-out" at school.

He's about as cute and sharp as nine-year-olds come.

Then there's Lexi, the one with the world's greatest smile.

Lexi isn't clingy, like Candice. In fact, she's just the opposite, most of the time. She plays a little hard to get, a trait I'm going to appreciate in her a bunch more when she gets to be a teenager.

Always running to get away.

Hiding.

Trying to get loose when she is finally caught.

One thing I've noticed, though: She always slips up at

least once. She always manages to get caught, just before it's time for me to leave. Then she'll flash that million dollar smile to let everybody know that she sure hated getting caught and won't let it happen again, if she can help it.

At least, not until next time.

Then there's the one some would say is my favorite, although I love them equally.

Austin.

Austin—since he was three, maybe younger—has sat with me at church. I take notes at church, always printing, never writing in cursive. I do that so he can lean over and read my notes and copy them in his notepad. I think I'm responsible as much as his first grade teacher and almost as much as his mama for teaching him how to write, right there at church since he was three. At least, I take credit for that.

And when he isn't taking notes in church he's singing at the top of his lungs. That boy, I tell you, can flat sing, and occasionally he'll hit the right notes, too.

So, on their ninth birthday—nine going on three as far as I'm concerned—I grabbed my bag of presents and headed over to make my delivery to my four best friends. Before I could get the car parked, Candice spotted me through the window, ran out the door and tackled me right there in the front yard, spraying me with kisses and delivering the world's greatest nine-year-old hugs.

Grantman heard the commotion and came and piled on, then Lexi, grinning from ear to ear, and, last, my note-taking, songbird-singing Austin.

We uncovered the pile a little later, and I delivered my gifts amid a recurrence of hugs and kisses. When I'd taken what mom and dad thought was my share of unusual punishment, I straightened myself up, got back in my car, and waved goodbye amid shouts of "I love you." (I think the kids were hollering, too.)

But I couldn't help—as I headed away—but to pause and say a little prayer to the good Lord.

Thanks for October 3.

October 3, 2000

Inspiration Point #10

When the fans on both sides of the football field stand up and cheer as a young man gallops in for the touchdown, you know you've just witnessed a rare inspirational point. It hasn't happened many times, but it happened to Jake in his last home high school football game…

JAKE WINS GAME NOBODY ELSE COULD

Jake's story skidded its way across the icy Ohio, braved the mountains of Kentucky, and waltzed across Tennessee to find its way to Georgia-land, via the storytelling I do every week in the *La Grange Daily News*.

Jake's story is another one of those with an unlikely hero—kind of like Chase Freeman, I guess.

Jake is a high school senior from a little town on the edge of Ohio, not far from the Kentucky line. He is a special student, limited mentally by a disease that makes learning difficult. Nonetheless, Jake has found his niche in the little town of McDermott and in its high school.

When he leaves home every morning, he tells his mom, "I'm going to work!" Then, at school, he puts his own name on the teachers' sign-in sheet, and the principal tells him to be sure to pick up his check before leaving that day.

His is a special story, indeed.

Jake also gets to participate in sports on a limited basis. That's where this heart-warming story comes from.

Last year as a junior, Jake got in *one* football game and kneeled the ball down harmlessly at the coach's command.

This year—a couple of weeks ago—his coach wanted

him to have that chance again in his team's last home game, Jake's last home game as a senior.

So Jake's coach, Coach Frantz, called Coach DeWitt from Waverly High and asked if it'd be all right if he put Jake in again, if the game wasn't close. He knew Waverly was a powerhouse team and that Jake might get a chance.

Coach DeWitt agreed.

And sure enough, that Friday night, Jake got his chance.

It wasn't just Jake's teammates cheering him. It was the other team, too.

With his team trailing 42-0 with only seconds remaining, Coach Frantz called time out and met with DeWitt at mid-field to make sure that nobody hurt Jake if he put him in.

"We'll do more than let him play," said DeWitt graciously, "We'll let him score!"

"Nah," said Frantz, "I'll just have him kneel the ball down. That will be enough."

So they put Jake in, handed the ball to him, and told him to kneel.

But Jake didn't kneel.

Jake went berserk. He started running around in the backfield. Coach Frantz yelled frantically from the sideline, "Jake, kneel the ball! Kneel the ball!"

But Jake wasn't hearing.

Jake just ran circles in the backfield, having the time of his life.

Finally, the players on the field hollered, "Jake, go score! Go score!" pointing to the goal line.

It wasn't just Jake's teammates. It was the *other* team, too.

In a moment, in a grand display of brotherhood, both teams directed Jake toward the goal line.

So Jake ran.

And ran.

Jake ran fifty yards for the score, with both teams escorting him, running along with him, encouraging him, praising him, loving him.

When Jake scored, both bands played their victory songs.

Both teams' cheerleaders yelled.

All the fans on both sides applauded and cheered.

Everybody from two towns high-fived and hugged Jake.

Because everybody was so excited, Jake thought he'd just won the game!

And in a way he had.

Actually, *everybody* won.

And, most importantly of all, Jake had his moment in the sun!

Run, Jake, run!

November 23, 2002

Inspiration Point #11

It was one of the most inspirational moments: Driving through the back streets of a Georgia-red-clay town not far from my home, and listening to an a cappella version of one of the great hymns, then realizing that when the songwriter penned the words, he must've had me in mind…

IT IS WELL WITH MY SOUL

Kneeling there beneath a thousand pines was the grand ol' Chattahoochee…

From my vantage point on the fourth floor of the nearby hospital, I could see the river for a mile winding its way through tall, elegant pines, flowing so peacefully it didn't look as if it had a worry in the world. A thousand pines, embedded in that deep, red, Georgia clay, stood by in honor and admiration of the majestic river.

And the river kneeled at their feet.

It was quite a sight.

I took all that in one recent July when I was home visiting Georgia. I drove up to the little town of Lanette, Alabama, to visit one of my great-aunts in the hospital. My Aunt Florence, Mama's baby sister, was there, too, so after we visited Aunt Katherine a while, the two of us escaped to a little waiting room in the corner of the hospital. While we sat there together, we could look out the window from that fourth or fifth hospital floor to that stunning view.

I could see the river for a mile winding its way through tall, elegant pines...

Long after the sun had turned the lights out on that magnificent image, I drove home alone, thinking of its grandeur. It was when I turned on the radio to keep me company on that lonely drive home, that I stumbled across some music that made me shake my head in wonder a bit more. It was a gospel music station, and an a cappella group was singing one of the great hymns:

"When peace like a river attendeth my way, when sorrows like sea billows roll, whatever my lot, thou hast taught me to say, It is well, it is well, with my soul."

The angel-like sound filling the night air was almost as awe-inspiring as the scene of the Chattahoochee I had seen earlier. I thought that for a fella's heart to be able to put those thoughts into words, he must have an uncanny ability to look through a dark night and see the next morning's dawn ahead. When Mr. H.G. Stafford wrote "It is Well," he must have been feeling some of the burdens that sometimes flow our way —or, he had known those things far too well in the past. Long after this night had faded into an inspiring memory, I learned that Mr. Stafford, indeed, understood "sorrows like sea billows" all too well.

We all probably can relate to the message: Regardless of our circumstance—whether it be a time that is as peaceful as the flowing of that grand ol' Chattahoochee that July evening, or whether sorrows like sea billows roll—no matter the situation, we can still sing with great confidence: "It is well, it is well, with my soul."

I like that.

When you can sing words like that, there's a feeling down deep inside that's as peaceful as the rolling of the majestic Chattahoochee on a calm Georgia night. Such a peace doesn't come from thinking about how awfully good we are. We all know that we aren't that good.

Nor does it come in our adding up all the good deeds and works we've done, because no amount of the work that we can do is enough to repay the debt we owe.

You understand.

The peace comes because—despite our nature and despite our shortcomings—He has taken all our sins and wrong turns and distant journeys far away from home and nailed them to a rugged tree on a little hill, allowing them to flow straight out of sight down that river where we were first immersed.

So that's the reason, regardless of where life has taken us, that we can sing with renewed confidence, as that a cappella group sang that Georgia night:

"It is well…it is well…it is well with my soul."

April 19, 2002

Inspiration Point #12

While growing up, going to church and playing basketball were probably the two things I did the most. I still do both. Over the past thirty years, no trip back home to Georgia was ever complete without dropping by the "Y" and teaching some of my old buddies there how to play the game—and, occasionally, being taught by *them*. The teacher who most inspired me—at least on one particular day—was a fella named Bubba Hill…

BUBBA INSPIRES INTENSE GAME OF DOMINOES

Luke is his name, but most of us call him Bubba.

Bubba Hill.

Bubba is a pretty decent basketball player from LaGrange, Georgia.

He played for LaGrange College back when everybody wore the Larry Bird shorts, way back before the three-point line.

Now, a couple of decades later, Bubba plays at the "Y" several times a week on his lunch hour with all the guys I play with when I come to town.

The problem with coming home to play with Bubba and the boys twice a year is that I'm not always in the best of shape, so sometimes I don't have my "game" with me. It's kind of like when you pack in a hurry. Sometimes you leave some things at home. I've found it's not good to be at the Y playing ball when your game is still in a drawer at home 750 miles away.

I hurried on down to the Y the first day I got to town to reunite with the boys and resume our rivalry and trash talking. We hadn't played very long before it dawned on me that my game hadn't come along. Plumb forgot to pack it. So I was struggling to guard anybody. Bubba hit a shot in my face from the wing one time, then drove by me and hit a Mario Ellie type runner in the lane the next.

My buddy Steve Sauter rebounded over the top of me and laid one up on me, leaving his elbow prints on my back. Ken Carter threw in one of his long left-handed three-pointers because I was too slow getting over to guard him. *Everybody* had a field day—David, Alan, Louie, even an old fella with a slow first move named Roger. Each took his turn scoring on me and making me look bad.

Things weren't any better on the offensive end of the floor, either. I bricked a shot from the wing. I shot an air ball from the corner. And—most embarrassing of all—I drove in with my left hand and had Bubba throw my shot over against the brick wall and then glare at me with a "That weak stuff may work in Texas but it won't fly here in Georgia" look.

It was painful. It was so bad that the normally mild-mannered and modest Bubba finally turned to me and said, "Coach, maybe you'd be better off goin' down the hall and playin' dominoes or somethin'."

Now, I don't blame Bubba so much for saying what he said. It's hard to blame a fella when he's right. In fact, I appreciate him for being up front and plain and outright and honest.

I thank him, too, for making me mad.

That's right.

He made me mad, and I turned right there in the mid-dle of the game and thanked him. I was mad because he

I lowered my head, drove to the basket, and laid a shot up with my right hand, just over Bubba's outstretched arm.

said the very thing I knew everybody else was thinking and just had too much Southern hospitality to say out loud. But I still have enough competitive juices flowing in these old bones that I wanted to do something about it. So, the next time down the floor I lowered my head, drove to the basket, and laid a shot up with my right hand, just over Bubba's outstretched arm.

Next time it was a three pointer from downtown over my good buddy Professor Paschal, a déjà vu moment from last summer when I hit the same shot for the game-winner just before I headed back to Texas.

Then it was a fade away three pointer over Carter from just this side of Callaway Gardens.

And, finally, for the game winner, with Bubba hanging all over my arm, I threw in a three-pointer from the shadow of the Georgia Dome and never even called a foul.

I appreciate Bubba and all the boys who were on the wrong end of those shots. They never got mad. Never kicked a trash can or anything. Never talked trash. In fact, as soon as that last rocket had landed softly and uttered its sweet swishing sound for all the boys to hear, Bubba calmly and gentlemanly said,

"Nice shot, Coach," then headed to the shower.

I was modest, too, because I knew I'd gotten a little lucky with a few of those missiles, so I didn't say anything myself. I let my good buddy Professor Paschal do my talking for me.

"I want to tell you this, Coach," said the professor as we were getting a drink at the water fountain, "that was one of the best games of dominoes I've seen in a long time."

March 24, 2001

Inspiration Point #13

Preacher Miller always stood up for what he believed, no matter what. But he knew it would take a mighty big man to walk up into that pulpit up in Kentucky one night back in the '50s. He knew there were guns in the audience, and those guns were gunning for him!…

PREACHER MILLER STANDS HIS GROUND IN KENTUCKY

Most of the time, storytelling is pretty easy for me, especially when the subject of Preacher Miller comes up...

But this time it wasn't.

When I got to the end, this time I had to pause. I didn't intend to, but I had to. I guess that moment of hesitation—that pause that I needed to let the emotions simmer a bit—reminded me that the *telling* of the story was a point of inspiration just as the story itself was.

Each year I give my students the task of sharing in front of the room the life of the person who has most influenced them.

To set the stage, I tell my own story.

My story takes me through several important people in my life, especially from the growing up years—Mama and Grandma, in particular—but I settle in on that *one* influence that shaped my character in his special way: the man who wet his pants night after night: Preacher Miller.

Among the many things that impressed me about the man was his courage, his faith to stand up for what he believed, no matter who "standing up" meant he'd be standing *against*. I've tried to hammer off a chip or two of that quality and edge it into myself, but I must say it's easier to write about than to do.

It was up in Kentucky back in the '50s that his faith and his courage and his "standing up" was put to the ultimate test.

Granddad went to preach up in the hills of Kentucky many times, and he knew the people there well. Folks up in those hills could be rough and mean. That's probably quite an understatement. But that put them in greater need of the gospel, and nobody was better equipped to deliver it than this Georgia preacher-man.

Brother Miller had many strong beliefs. One that he held was that a person should not be a part of the organization of the Masons. The Masons back then were a pretty powerful group and could lay a penalty on your head in the worst way if you stepped out of line. That element—along with a few of their other practices—was why the preacher felt the organization went against the Book.

The problem was, about half the folks in this backwoods church up in Kentucky were Masons. Since he believed if he saw any fault in somebody that it was his duty to bring it to the forefront, Preacher Miller announced one night in his booming, rafter-shaking voice,

"Tomorrow night, we're goin' to the word of God to examine the *Masons!*"

Obviously, that announcement didn't fly too well among the half of the congregation who were Masons, so after the service they went up to him and warned him not to do it. He listened to the warning, but he knew a greater

Authority told him "not to shun to declare the *whole* counsel of God."

He was one night away from jumping into the "*whole* counsel."

Head first.

The next day would be the day of reckoning in Preacher Miller's life. His life would be threatened, and he would walk into a church building with folks packing something that could help them carry that threat out.

The afternoon before the sermon, some of those rough Kentuckian farmers met him at his motel and warned him once more against preaching that sermon. One big strong fella sent him a warning by reaching out and bending his tie tack. Preacher Miller, as anyone who knew him knows, always wore a suit and tie, regardless of what time of day it was. This time it would get a bit dusty. Another brute of a man went up to him and pushed him and his starched suit down and threw a few snarling insults toward him. I guess he thought this would discourage Preacher Miller from walking into that pulpit that night with that sermon in mind.

Preacher Miller got up as their car drove away, dusted off his dark suit, then set himself for what he had to do, kind of like Elijah did when he had to go face to face with King Ahab.

That night that ol' country church was packed. Regular church members were not the only ones there, either. News had flown through the town and countryside, bringing folks in from all around.

On the one side of that church that night were those who supported the Masons. On the other side were those agin', as some folks in the South say.

A sword divided.

But both sides had one thing in common. Both groups had folks who had come for blood. They were carrying guns inside their jackets, and they weren't afraid to use them.

Preacher Miller remembered that scene for as long as he lived.

But guns or no guns, the preacher had taken his stand and would have to maintain that stand like Elijah.

When the singing was done, Preacher Miller, tall and strong, made his way to the pulpit just as he had done that whole week, just as he did several thousand times in his fifty-plus years of preaching.

He got to the pulpit, scanned that ravenous crowd, and bellowed out his sermon topic with that loud, raspy voice just as he had always done, both in peace and in war.

"Brothers, sisters, and friends," he began, "I may not walk out of this pulpit the same way I walked in, but tonight, like I announced last evenin', I'm goin' to preach on the Masons!"

Despite the benevolent work the Masons performed, they would have to withstand the scrutiny of the Scriptures through and through that night.

So Preacher Miller—deep in the backwoods of Kentucky—stood his ground and preached and sweated and quoted Scripture for the better part of an hour.

Amazingly, both sides of that church building sat and listened without disturbance.

There were no fights, no gunfire.

The only commotion in the whole place was the preacher's shaking of the rafters with his courage and quotation of Scriptures.

For some reason—I don't know why, and neither did the preacher—nobody pulled a gun to make his opinion known. Preacher Miller, and the truth he believed in, won that battle without a shot being fired.

When it was all said and done, he got in his car and drove back to Georgia, all in one piece. But he said a half dozen set of car lights escorted him all the way to the Tennessee line, at which point they wheeled around and headed back home.

I always admired Preacher Miller for his courage back there, years before I was even born. And because I've admired him so, most of the thousands of students I've taught the past two decades have heard the story you may be hearing for the first time.

Thirty-five or forty years after his great stand in Kentucky, Preacher Miller would take his last journey up to the pulpit to proclaim the gospel with a rare vigor and intensity. The giant of a man, nearing the age of eighty, had to succumb to the dictates of time.

Along with many of his heroics, I had to share that part of the story with my students. And even though he died in December of '89, sometimes that part of the story gets a bit hard, especially when I had to see him at the end as only a shadow of the man he once was.

So I had to summon a little smile at that point of the story to drive away that lump that had crept into my throat.

But the look of admiration I've always had—that remained. Nothing could change what I felt:

Preacher Miller was then, and always will be, a giant of a man.

February 1, 2003

Inspiration Point #14

Grandma is getting old, and I know there are times her angels get to swooping mighty low. But I'm glad to say there's another flock of angels out there, too, who keep shooing them away. Those angels are looking out for somebody else!…

NOT QUITE READY FOR THE ANGELS' SWOOP

No matter how hard I try, I can't get ready for the angels to swoop down and take away Grandma!…

I know they're coming before too long, but getting ready for that day is hard to do.

Some people, I guess, don't even believe in angels.

But I do.

I don't mean just the flesh and blood kind like Grandma, either. We all know about those kinds and have had our lives touched by them.

But I believe in the other kind, too, the ones who float overhead and whack mean folks over the head when they try to mess with us.

Now, this belief hasn't sneaked up on me all at once. It has kind of evolved as I've sat back and watched life. No greater evidence of angels exists than the fact that I've remained in one piece through my forty-something absent-minded years.

But just the last couple of days—since I've arrived here in La Grange on spring break—I've learned a little more about these angels. As I write this, I'm sitting at

Grandma's kitchen table, and she's making potato soup (and showing me how it's done). Even though her eyes and ears are wearing down (after all, she turned ninety-three the seventeenth of February), her mind has been as sharp as ever.

That is, until recently.

It's not that she's losing it. She has just started hearing voices the last couple of months. We sat at the table over a bowl of homemade tomato soup last night, and she told me about it. She'd hear some nice things, and then she'd also hear some arguing and carrying on.

"At least I know things aren't quite right," she said.

That's true. To be honest, even though I don't normally hear voices, I sometimes do some strange things that I try to lay off on being old—except I'm only half Grandma's age, and the only ones who buy my excuses any more are my students who actually think I *am* old.

So, I'm not overly alarmed at these voices Grandma's hearing. In fact, sometimes they may even prove to be a bit soothing.

"Stevie, d'you hear that?" Grandma said, as we sat at the table.

"What, Grandma?"

"That song."

And then she started singing to me what she was hearing in her head: *"And He walks with me and He talks with me. And He tells me I am his own…"*

There at the table eating tomato soup, she was hearing "In the Garden" in her head.

That can't be all bad.

I know some folks who'd pay for a gift like that. She's hearing angelic music, and all I could hear was a train honking its head off half a mile away.

So, last night, me and my ninety-three-year-old grandma and some angels overhead sat at the table singing "In the Garden" together. It was quite a scene.

All of this is beginning to make sense to me. The angels are giving Grandma songs of peace in her twilight years. But something stumped me. I understand about the good angels singing to Grandma, but I had a bit of trouble figuring out about all the arguing and carrying on she's been hearing.

Then it hit me. It came to me like a jagged fire bolt from heaven.

All that arguing's coming from *my* angels.

You see, at ninety-three, Grandma and I know that time for her is streaming by pretty fast, kind of like that train that zoomed by behind her house while we were talking last night. So, some of those voices Grandma is hearing may be her sweet angels making preparations to swoop down and take her away.

That's where *my* angels come in. I think my angels picked up on the plot and had to step in and put a firm angelic foot down.

You understand.

My angels have a job to do, too, you know—and watching out for *me* is no easy task! Anybody'll tell you that. In doing their job, there's this one little thing my angels have figured out when it comes to Grandma:

My heart's not quite ready for her angels to swoop down just yet.

March 15, 2003

Inspiration Point #15

Sometimes folks take a wrong turn along the way and have a hard time making it back to the main road. Such it was with a man on a midnight train, headed…nowhere. But there was a nearby train, and my hope is that one day—when that train rolls into the station—a little girl who has his blood running in her veins will be waiting…

MIDNIGHT TRAIN HEADED THE WRONG DIRECTION

Oh, no, there's no mistaking this train ride for the midnight train to Georgia...

It was more like a midnight train to nowhere.

At least, for now.

My brother Wayne and I took the train to downtown Dallas to watch a basketball game not long ago. It was after the game when we boarded the train and plopped in our seats to head back home that we saw him.

He was a pretty ordinary looking guy, as ordinary as they come on a train that late at night. I think I was the only really ordinary looking guy there. I wasn't even all that sure about Wayne.

As I sat in a seat facing the fella, he looked fifty, but it turned out he was only thirty-something. It kind of hit me hard when I realized he was quite a bit younger than me. He had sandy hair and a three or four day old beard, and he had a hard life written all over him.

By the time the train started pulling out to head toward Fort Worth, we had started a conversation with the man. His story didn't surprise me.

He had just gotten out of jail that night. He had gotten picked up on some long-time traffic violation that he couldn't pay.

He had no home, was just heading to Fort Worth to spend the night at a homeless shelter.

He was a bricklayer by trade. But because he had no tools, his most recent job was laboring until he could afford to buy his tools. Knowing that trade myself, I was able to pick up that he had a pretty good knowledge of bricklaying. He hoped to hook up the next day with a bricklaying outfit he used to work for in Fort Worth.

He was not married, but he had been at one time. His ex-wife lives in New Orleans.

"Do you have any kids?" I asked.

"One," he said, "I have a daughter who's 13. She lives in New Orleans with her mama. I haven't seen her in a year and a half."

"That's tough," I said with a grimace.

The train seemed to agree, because just about that time it screeched its brakes as it neared the end of the line.

"Let me tell you what I'd do, for what it's worth," I said, the train crawling the last hundred yards to the depot. "They have brick jobs in New Orleans just the same as they do in Fort Worth. I think I'd find the first train to New Orleans and get aboard and do whatever it takes to get to know my little girl."

"Yeah," he said, "that wouldn't be a bad thing to do."

The train came to a halt, its signal that our visit was finished. We headed for the door, and Wayne pulled out five dollars and gave it to the man.

I just said, "Don't forget New Orleans, now."

He nodded his head.

Outside in the drizzle, we watched the train pull away, carrying our new friend.

When that train stops—one day—the sound of jazz will be coming from the depot.

I hope.

September 14, 2002

Inspiration Point #16

It was quite a scene when a young man who bears my name walked across the stage to end his high school career in 1998. It was the same spring our four quadruplet butterflies stomped across the kindergarten stage themselves. You met the quads earlier on our hike, but they were nine then. Now they're five. You'll still recognize them, and you'll be inspired as I was when they came to the stage. There are two scenes here—in perfect juxtaposition—and there's a young eagle accompanied by four butterfly comrades…

KEYS TO REACHING HIGH AND TOUCHING THE SKY

Pride swelled way down deep inside me when my quadruplet graduates and a young man named Steven walked across the stage recently.

Actually they didn't walk. They flew.

At least, my four buddies Austin, Grant, Candice and Lexi *believed* they could fly when they put on their caps and gowns for the first time, marched with pride into that Lorena, Texas, gymnasium, sang with vigor, "I Believe I Can Fly," then sailed across the gym floor proudly to receive their diplomas.

I had a little lump in my throat that day as I watched them growing up. It's a proud day when little ones take that big step across the stage and move from the cocoon called kindergarten to the butterfly garden of first grade.

As they sang that song, I had no doubt that at such an age of innocence these four blonde-headed bundles of joy really could fly high and really could touch the sky.

But they weren't alone. The fifth one had wings, too.

Having graduated kindergarten twelve years ahead of the quads, a special young man named Steven had reached the next stage himself. He left his own cocoon, just before the quads would leave theirs. It's just that his was high school.

I knew that he, like they, would soon be reaching for the sky in a big way himself. I had no doubt that he would get there, too, because I had watched him flutter his wings for all of his eighteen years, and I watched him reach the sky skillfully, not unlike a youthful eagle.

I know him well. He carries not only my first name but my last as well. But we call him Mal.

To make sure that all five of my buddies will learn what they need to know to help them fly high outside the cocoon, I offer these little bits of advice. They may be a bit over the head of the four little butterflies, but they'll eventually grow. As they do, they'll figure out that some of these thoughts will be useful.

And the young eagle I know as my son also will need to master some of these elements. They'll help him add strength to his wings so he can soar to the dreams way up in the sky that he already sees.

So here's my advice to those five, and to all of you, and to me:

Put the Lord first in all things.

Believe in yourself.

Be the most positive and enthusiastic person you know.

Smile.

Learn people's names and call them by their names.

Never be called out on strikes. Go down swinging.

Hold your girlfriend's or boyfriend's hand as often as you can.

Control your dreams. Don't let your dreams control you.

Watch funny movies.

Read the Bible every day.

Follow the Bible closely, not adding to, not taking from.

Choose a profession where you can help others.

Do unto others as you would have them do unto you.

Make sure the person you look to marry is a friend.

Marry for love.

Say "Thank you."

Say "Please."

Own a dog. (Ah, I miss ol' Pee Wee. I'll have to tell you about him sometime. He was like Chico, just with a little more attitude.)

Say "I love you" every day.

Hug.

Take a stand for what you think is right.

Say "Yes ma'am" and "Yes sir!"

Open the door for the person behind you.

Pray.

Put family before job.

Learn to work on your car. (Okay, so I can't do that. Doesn't mean *you* can't!)

Learn to do carpenter work.

Walk thirty minutes a day.

Take a family vacation even if you have to borrow money for it.

Make sure you have a friend in Jesus.

Learn to handle adversity.

Watch "Andy Griffith" (and learn to nip life in the

bud, "nip it in the bud!")

Listen to your favorite music in the mornings.

Watch as many sunrises and sunsets as possible. (Make sure at least one of those is from Bromide Hill.)

Take Vitamin C.

Hang a basketball goal at your house.

Value your friends, your reputation—better yet, your *character*—your parents, and, someday, your children.

Read my column every week—and read all my books, too, if you don't mind.

Last of all—and most importantly—the real key to flying high and touching the sky is this:

Wait upon the Lord.

"But they that wait upon the Lord shall…soar with wings as eagles" (Isaiah 40:31).

That's the best advice I know to give to my young eagle and our four little butterfly friends as together they reach for the sky.

June 1998

Inspiration Point #17

You'll never hear anything more inspiring than the four-part harmony of quadruplet ten-year-olds spontaneously joining together in song. Packed tightly in the car on one of our many excursions together, they erupted out of nowhere, a mile or two from their home and the end of our night out. The harmony of the setting sun and western sky in the distance paled in comparison…

FOUR-PART HARMONY

Quadruplets grow up four times faster, at least that's the way it seems.

One year they were two, then they were graduating from kindergarten, and now they're telling me they're ten years old, or something crazy like that.

The truth is they're not a bit different to me than when they were three.

Austin's still the proper little preacher man.

Lexi still flashes a brilliant smile.

Candice is still as sweet as her name.

And Grantman's still the clown.

But something has changed, and it's something a little hard to take: Now, instead of seeing my little quartet several times a week, I have to settle for once every month or so as I've moved ninety miles north since their last birthday.

"Why'd you leave us?" asked Lexi in her innocence.

"Well, I, uh…" I stammered, trying to be delicate, "I have a, uh, a great teaching and coaching job where I moved to."

"Yeah," she said without hesitation, "but we're more important than a job."

Out of the mouths of babes.

I didn't argue, but I did marvel just a bit.

But what we've lost in quantity, we kind of make up for in quality. I picked my four fans up last month, and we headed out to a unique world with no cares and no worries. Not many of us experience that little piece of heaven much anymore, but the Lord is good and lets us go up to the mountaintop every now and then to get a glimpse of the good times. Kind of like what we're doing right now on our little journey together.

I must say that when the quads and I reached the mountaintop, the view was pretty special:

There's a white mustache just above Lexi's brilliant smile, derived from a sloppily-eaten ice cream cone.

There's Austin throwing a perfect strike on his way to an even 100 game of bowling—then shrugging it off with nothing but a little smile and a "Nothin' to it" expression on his face.

There's Grant knocking on the girl's bathroom door, while Lexi and Candice are taking a little potty break at the taco place and hollering out "Room Service!" for all to hear.

There's the four of them running back to me at the booth in exuberance, telling the story, each one doing so in their own special way.

There's Candice holding my hand at the playground as we watch the others swing and slide, run and sweat, seeing if they can set a record for combining sand with hair, clothes, and shoes.

There's Grant and Austin at the end of a rough slide, falling all over each other and the ground simultaneously, amidst laughter, moans, and groans.

There's Grant, finding the only book in all of Barnes and Noble that is equipped with a microphone, doing his very best Elvis impression to the entertainment of all the nearby patrons down at the store for a quiet evening of reading.

There are the four, standing side by side on Waco's grand Suspension Bridge posing for a picture: Austin in calm assurance, Lexi sporting her magazine cover smile and Candice her sheepish grin, and Grant acting like a monkey.

Then there are the four, together again, fulfilling a request for a song as we rounded the last turn before home. It was an instant blending of four voices completely in tune. It was as if a chorus of angels had suddenly emerged to lead us down the last road to home.

That—along with some big-time hugs at the end— marked the conclusion of a perfect evening of smiles and laugher and hugs and fun. Just me and four ten-year-olds in a night of complete harmony.

Ah, I think it was four-part harmony at its best.

October 6, 2001

Inspiration Point #18

I met another favorite "quartet" of mine way back in 1974, not long after my own personal trek across high school's stage. My buddy Ace introduced me to the music of the Statler Brothers that summer, and my life has never been the same. There have been many journeys since then—some way down in the valley and some up high to the mountaintop. But through it all— through the changes and the growing up—one constant has remained: the music of four friends from Virginia…

THE STATLERS, THE SHENANDOAH VALLEY, AND MEMORIES

Riding through the Shenandoah Valley in 2003 flooded me with memories, taking me all the way back to the summer of 1974. That was the summer Harold, Jimmy, Phil and Don popped into my life. Actually it was Phil, Harold, *Lew*, and Don at first, and Jimmy would replace Lew in the early '80s.

My buddy Ace introduced me to these four gentlemen known as the Statler Brothers while we were living in a little shack in a not-so-good-part of Dallas right after the two of us had graduated high school. On some lonely and balmy Dallas summer night, Ace sometimes would pull out an eight-track tape of the Statlers while we were lying around the little house whining about girls or whimpering about the muscles we'd pulled playing a little one-on-one over at the gym earlier in the day.

Those were the good times—and simple.

It was that same summer, almost thirty years ago, that

I fell in love with the Statlers' music.

For thirty years now their songs have served as a melodious backdrop to many of life's breathtaking snapshots: Walking innocently down the aisle, holding two little angels in my arms and realizing these were my own, and just growing up.

The Statlers were about as much a part of our lives as going to church and walking the kids to school and riding bicycles together and eating supper at the table at night.

That's why I was so honored back in August when I visited the hometown of the Statlers up in Staunton, Virginia, and their office, which—since the boys hung up their cleats last October—is only a small brick building on the outskirts of town.

As I made my way home from Staunton after soaking in the simple scenes around their offices, I plugged in the CD for their farewell concert held last October in Salem, Virginia.

It was quite a scene.

Listening to the four-part harmony as I had done for three decades—from "I'll Go to my Grave Loving You" to "Amazing Grace."

Driving through the Shenandoah Valley with the towering blue-shaded Shenandoah Mountains painted in the distance to the east and to the west.

All of that through slightly misty eyes.

I'm not sure exactly what it was that made that drive a bit emotional. Probably many things.

It was having just left my son 1500 miles from home up in New Jersey. He's a long way from home chasing a dream "like he always wanted to"—kind of like a baseball pitcher the Statlers once sang about—meanwhile leaving a little void in his mama and daddy's hearts.

It was thinking back to the time when I first heard the Statlers sing "Daddy" in 1974 and wondering why my own daddy had to leave me before I really got to know 'im.

It was remembering when the Statlers first sang "How Great Thou Art." I listened to their elegant version of the great hymn many a morning as I was heading out to the brick job in the late '70s to support two young children and a wife the best way I knew how.

It was thinking back—as a result of the nostalgic tones that emerge from their songs—to yesteryear, to the many days that have come and gone: the victories and defeats, the mistakes and banners, the joys and sadness, the exhilarating hikes up the mountain and the journeys way down low in those valleys. Some of those journeys carried us down as low as bass singer Harold himself can sing, and others would send us so high on the mountain that young Jimmy Fortune would have to tip-toe to hit a note to match.

I guess the emotion came from wondering whose music would inspire and carry us the rest of the way, as we climb a few more steep hills that loom ahead and descend gingerly—hands on each others' shoulders—down the slopes that I know are bound to come.

I know I can plug in a Statler song any time I want—maybe "Maple Street Memories" or "Class of '57"—and lean back and pretend it's 1974 all over again.

Ah, things really were simple back then.

I'm sure the Statlers themselves would agree.

September 27, 2003

Inspiration Point #19

It was only a memory of a day in junior high when Mike Cosper and I strapped on the boxing gloves…but it became more when his brother Butch wrote me a letter twenty-five years after Mike died…

STRAPPIN' ON THE GLOVES IN '69

Strapping on the gloves in '69 almost made me a man. It could have stripped every ounce of pride I had in my 12-year-old veins, too—but it didn't…

This story takes me way back.

Seventh grade.

West Side Junior High School.

This would become both a moment of truth and a point of inspiration, mainly because I survived it with at least a little thread of dignity.

The lot fell upon me one scary seventh-grade day to do something I didn't want to do: to fight. Sometimes you do what you have to do if you want to hold your head high as you walk the junior high halls, even when you aren't fully equipped for the task.

You see, I wasn't big back then.

I wasn't mean.

I wasn't tough.

I wasn't even a fighter. For that matter, I wasn't a lover, either. I was nothing, just a regular ol' seventh-grade kid who walked around the halls trying to survive and mind his own business and not get beat up.

But none of that stopped the big test from coming.

I walked into P.E. class one day, and coach Sanders had a plan. I don't know where he conjured the plan up or why. But somewhere between the day before and that fateful day he decided he wanted two boys from the P.E. class to strap the boxing gloves on and fight.

That, of course, was something that nobody could get away with nowadays. But back then, you could do those kinds of things, plus play a violent game of dodge ball on rainy days that'd send you back to class bruised and sore with red spots all over your body.

And back then all seventh graders were eligible to encounter the wrath of a teacher's paddle.

Always long.

Always wide.

Usually with holes in it to add an extra degree of pain when it made contact.

I was one of the lucky ones, I guess, who didn't miss out on the enjoyment of any of those things, including the boxing matches.

I don't know why Coach Sanders decided that day to do what he did. I don't remember his ever doing it again. He just did it once. He chose two boys, and one was me.

The other was Mike Cosper.

There were several things bad about his choosing Mike Cosper. One, he was littler than me. That may not sound like such a bad thing to you now, but when you're in the seventh grade, that's a bad thing.

You see, for a seventh-grader, the key thing is pride.

It's dignity.

It's being able to hold your head up when you walk into the science lab or the lunchroom.

The truth of the matter is this: If you get beat up by

somebody littler than you, then you have to go through the entire seventh grade with your head bowed low, maybe even through the rest of junior high school. You can't hold your head up in biology or math or the lunchroom or the hallway or the playground or homeroom.

Nowhere.

So I've had this little chip on my shoulder toward Coach Sanders ever since then for picking Mike Cosper for me to box. It was all right that he picked me out of all the boys in the seventh grade. I could live with that. But for the past thirty years I've had a hard time dealing with his picking somebody littler than me to fight. It was a no-win situation.

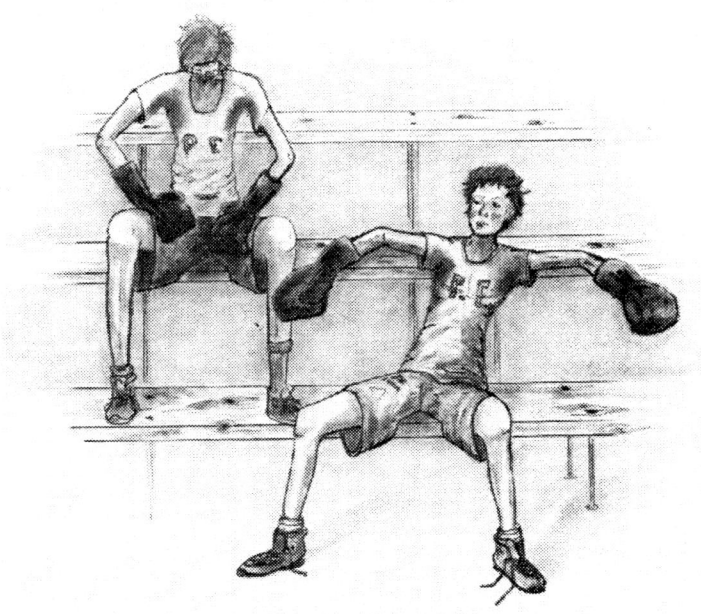

If you get beat up by somebody littler than you, you have to go through the entire seventh grade with your head bowed low.

Another bad thing about having to fight Mike was that while Mike was little, he was tough. Unlike me, Mike didn't have a bit of fat on his body. He was like a little ball of string: wound tight and tough. There were a lot of guys bigger than me that I would much rather have fought, because at least then I could've responded in the lunchroom, "Yeah, but I gave 'im a good fight."

The other thing about Mike that made me not want to fight him was that he was a nice guy. He was fairly quiet, didn't bother anybody, didn't get into too much trouble. He was just an easy-going guy, and I knew that fighting him I wouldn't have that added uummp in my punch that would occur naturally if I were fighting Buster or Boatwright or one of the other smartalecks walking the seventh-grade hall. (Sorry, Boatwright, I had to throw you in there, even though seventh grade was a long time ago. But we kind of made up at lunch thirty years later when we bumped into each other at Mike's Grill on Main Street in the heart of La Grange. You're all right now, in my book. I still think you should've picked up the tab, though.)

There were more than a few fellas at West Side in the seventh grade that I would've liked to've rared back and punched right in the nose with that red pair of boxing gloves and knocked them all the way back to Mrs. Goforth's third grade class. But most of those guys were circled around Mike and me to hoot and holler and carry on and cheer for one or the other of us, more than likely Mike, because, as I said, Mike was a nice guy that everybody liked, and I was kind of a wise guy, myself.

So most of the rest of the seventh grade boys gathered around and made their bets as Mike and I strapped on the gloves. Then, right there in the West Side Junior High gym, we touched gloves and began the best fight of 1969, maybe even the entire decade.

We fought like we were bitter enemies.

We swung with the vigor of a jealous boyfriend.

We fought with determination.

We jabbed and dodged and zigged and zagged as we swung.

We threw hooks and upper cuts and body punches and nose punches and—by the end—just blind punches until our little seventh-grade arms felt like they were going to fall slap off.

But there was no quit in us, not these two little seventh graders. I thought Coach Sanders would never blow the whistle. My arms weighed a hundred pounds, but I kept on swinging—and so did Cosper—until finally the whistle sounded and Coach mercifully put us out of our misery.

I'll never forget what happened next. Coach put the rest of the class through a grueling physical exercise work-out called the "wheelbarrow," while Mike and I sat in the bleachers and watched. Two lightweight boxers, two seventh-grade gladiators, two battlefield buddies, two champions who had just fought to an even draw—there we sat, side by side with sweat-soaked clothes, both anxious for the bell to ring, anxious to go to lunch so we could do what the other eighteen wished they could do:

Walk into the lunchroom with heads held high.

I don't guess there's anything in the world better for a seventh-grader than that.

January 20, 2001

Can we pause here a moment and let me tell you the rest of the story?

That was the way I wrote Mike Cosper's story back in 2001.

I didn't know the rest of the story would come later.

Years ago—long before I sat down to recall this junior high memory of me and my friend Mike Cosper—my cousin Mark Bailey, who still lived in La Grange at the time, told me that Mike had died out of season only a few years from high school. Sadly, life somehow became too difficult for him, and he brought it to an end.

Upon reading this story in the newspaper, his brother Butch wrote me a letter. His message was short.

"Thanks for the memory."

That was all he wrote.

Sometimes little things—like the strapping on of the gloves in junior high school or the writing of a short note—take on special importance.

That's how I feel about the fight of '69.

I think Butch now agrees.

We've come to the top of Inspiration Point now, and there are several more stories I want to tell you as we look out over those tall pines in the distance. I've enjoyed your coming along with me so far, but I'm especially glad you're with me now. I need to share the final chapter of one of life's great books.

Inspiration Point #20

On October 4, 2003, the angels came and gently ungripped my hand so that they could take away my own personal guardian angel. She had watched out for and served me for the most part of the last half of a century, and I went home faithfully to her table of cornbread and butter-milk for thirty years. Going home won't ever be the same…

HAVE THE CORNBREAD READY, GRANDMA: I'LL BE COMING HOME BEFORE YOU KNOW IT!

Thirty years and one day after Mama ended her journey, the angels came to usher another giant from my life.

On October 6, 2003—not a hundred feet from where Mama's memorial is—we laid our sweet angel to rest. It was exactly thirty years to the day that we had buried Mama, Grandma's own precious daughter.

When somebody like Grandma takes that grand journey, it's a wonderful thing. It's an occasion of glory, not as it is with some others.

She had lived almost 94 years. She had labored and served and cooked and nursed and taught and read and loved—she had done all that every step of the way. But the last few months, she was unable to do many of those things. Still she was so sweet and patient as her son Raymond and daughter Little Florence served her the best they could. It's just that she was a stranger to *being* served, and they knew it.

So her bags had been packed since before the spring flowers bloomed, and she was waiting at the dock for the angels to come.

They came Saturday, October 4.

She had been trying to pull up anchor and take this grand journey for about twenty-four hours, but each time that she seemed to be close, the family would get emotional, so she'd rally again. She seemed to be waiting for *them*—Little Florence and Raymond and a host of others. She was waiting for them to let her go quietly into that good night.

So when the time came, they were ready. The children and some of the grandchildren and friends from church gathered around her bed. I waited by the phone 725 miles away, waiting for the call I knew I'd never be ready to get.

But they had been prepared. They gathered around and held her hand and sang "Nearer my God to Thee."

They were ready, so Grandma knew she could go.

She opened her eyes, something she hadn't done much the past few days. The wonder in her eyes told them she was seeing something far more wonderful than what our earthly eyes can see. She was seeing the angels gather in the near distance, gathering to take her home.

As they sang, she raised her arm in the air suddenly.

It was an amazing scene.

She raised her arm, I know, to welcome the angels who had made their descent to take her away.

Then her arm fell, and she was gone.

Her ship had pulled anchor, and she was setting off on that grand journey.

The angels had come, and, with all the gentleness this

I'll be coming home to see you again, and I know you'll meet me at the door.

sweet lady deserved, they carried her away to the safe arms of Jesus.

For thirty years since Mama left, Grandma was both my grandma and my mama. She was my angel and my compass. Going home to Grandma was about the best thing I ever did. She always waited for me at the door with open arms and with a table full of love.

Ah, I love you, Grandma, and now as I begin to realize that I must finish my journey without you, my heart is a little heavy.

But don't worry: Before too long, I know I'll be coming home to see you again, and—as always—I know you'll meet me at the door.

Be sure to have the cornbread ready when I get there.

October 11, 2003

Looking out across the valley beneath a moment more…

I'm so thankful, my good hiking friends, that you chose to stay close by as we shared this story from the peak of Inspiration Point. It was a special privilege for me to tell it.

There are few more scenic views down a ways, and we'll work our way toward them. But maybe we should rest again here by this tall pine before we go any further. We can just look out for a bit and enjoy the breeze. In a bit, after we rest, and after we make our way to a few more inspiring views, I want to share one more little glimpse of Grandma.

Inspiration Point #21

It takes an earthquake to inspire some people. In the case of Jacob Job, the earthquake came in the form of a rattlesnake—*and* the most curious prayer Jacob Job ever heard a preacher pray…

PREACHER'S PRAYER RATTLES MOUNTAINEERS

Unusual prayers can rattle you...

They might even make God clear His throat.

That's the way it was with this one prayer that Preacher Miller told me what seemed like a hundred times as we traveled down a lonely, dark highway on the way to preach in a distant state.

Traveling with Preacher Miller as a boy, often late at night—perhaps beating down the pavement on Highway 80 between Selma, Alabama, and Meridian, Mississippi, on the way to a little western town in Texas where he would be preaching—he'd wake me up many a time slapping his leg and humming some song in his gruff old raspy but powerful voice. I'd wipe the sleep from my eyes, lean up, and watch the white dashes fly by for a while. After a minute, I'd say:

"Grandaddy, tell me one of your stories."

There was always a favorite of mine I'd ask for:

"Tell me the one 'bout the ol' sinful man from Kentucky whose son got bit by a rattlesnake and called for the preacher, and the preacher came and prayed that crazy prayer."

Preacher Miller would churn it over in his mind for what seemed like a hundred miles, and just when I was about to fade back into sleep, he'd jump into the story. If I wasn't already fully awake, that'd wake me up for sure. As I said, it was my favorite.

With his loud, raspy voice, he'd boom out...

Up in the hills of 'ol Kentuck,
meanest place that ere was struck,
There lived a man named Jacob Job,
the meanest man on this ol' globe.
He feared not God nor cared for man,
'cept his wild and wicked clan.

He had six boys, both big and bad,
that followed right behind their dad.
They drank that wildcat whiskey down,
and painted red the country town.

He had six girls—
big, buxom gals,
Who danced and frolicked on the hills,
and sometimes tippled at the stills.

One day an awful rattlesnake bit the oldest boy,
big wicked Jake.
And through his veins a virus flew,
he's bound to die, what shall we do?

They sent a runner to the town
to haste and fetch the parson down.
A preacher of John Wesley's band,
as good as any in the land.

He prayed a wondrous, curious prayer,
in words of faith both rich and rare.
If to heaven it reached or not,
one thing for sure it hit the spot.

He prayed,

"Oh, God, we thank thee for this snake,
that thou hast sent to bite ol' Jake.
To fetch him off of his high horse,
and lead him to the Saviour's cross.

"Oh, God, he never would repent,
until this blessed snake was sent.
He would not mend his wicked ways,
'til kind providence struck today.

"And, now, O God, the great I AM,
please send another'n to bite ol' Sam.
Send the meanes' ones you make,
O, please, we need more rattlesnakes.

"Send chicken snakes to bite the gals,
and all their dancing, wicked pals.
There's mama Job, she needs one, too,
perhaps a copperhead would do.

"Then send the biggest'n on the globe,
to bite ol' daddy Jacob Job.
And, now, O God, before too late,
please hurry up these rattlesnakes,
And save this ol' Kentucky state.

We ask it all for Jesus' sake.
AAAA-MEN!"

And with that "AAAA-Men!" the Georgia preacher
would let out a boisterous laugh that'd make his shoulders
move up and down, and keep on driving down the road.
Now satisfied, I'd smile and lean on back against the door
to try to get a little sleep.

October 1998

Inspiration Point #22

Being the baby in the family is one of the hardest ways to grow up. But you do get inspired pretty much every day of your life that-a-way, I can promise you that. Big brothers inspire you to do lots of things, such as stay out of their way as best you can, or run crying to Mama and Daddy a couple of times a day when you get smacked in the nose, or hide under the bed when you hear those two mean big brothers coming. Sometimes they encourage you to just keep your mouth shut "if you know whut's good for yer." But most of all, they inspire you to keep your feet on the ground at all cost! Read on, you'll see what I mean...

IF YOU DON'T LIKE ME THE WAY I AM, BLAME MY TWO BROTHERS

Vivian Rowe saved my life back in 1961.

That's why I live today to tell and laugh about it.

But the funniest things in life aren't too funny at the time they happen. I know it wasn't very funny back then when my big brothers let their imaginations get carried away, and I would be the one to pay for it.

The kind of stunts they would pull led Daddy to say, "They did *what?*" whenever I'd run hollering and screaming to him a couple of times a day.

These, uh, acts of imagination were so bad that, even today, I've officially decided that I'm not responsible for any faults that I have, or—should I say—*all* the faults I have.

I've tried to be noble about it for all these years and take responsibility the way a man's supposed to, but—after further review—I think I have to lay the blame somewhere else and throw nobility out the window. I think my therapist would agree.

For those who know me best, when I tell you where the blame lies, at least some of you are going to say, "Well, I can see a little bit of truth in that," even if you don't wholeheartedly go along with my new position.

I can tell you where the blame for my faults lies in two words:

Clifford Timothy and Douglas Wayne.

(You see, I told you the damage was bad!)

Those fellas are my two big brothers. One reason I lay so much blame on them is that their sole purpose for existence from the day I was born until I was seventeen or eighteen was somehow to get me to run away from home. They were tired of sharing the jello and the pudding and the ice cream in the icebox and the peanut butter and—above all— a bedroom.

So they figured that if they could aggravate me and mistreat me enough that—sooner or later—I'd pack up my bags, throw my knap sack over my shoulder, and head to California or somewhere, somewhere far enough away that I was no longer a threat to the chocolate pudding.

Of all the imaginative things these two hoodlums came up with, the most famous is their attempt to send me to the moon.

When I was about five or six, I don't know exactly because this is one snapshot of my life I've tried to avoid reviewing when time comes to flip through the photo album of my mind. I just know I was young, probably quite a bit younger than the chinaberry tree that you're about to hear about.

Tim and Wayne—who would have been pushing nine and ten—must have thought up this particular adventure on one of those slow summer days. I don't know what made them think of it, because it would have been around 1961,

Tim and Wayne tied me to that Chinaberry tree limb and were ready to send me to the moon!

and that was a good eight years before Neal Armstrong did what they were thinking about getting me to do.

But they got the idea that they would send me to the moon. So they tied me to the limb of the chinaberry tree that stands in the back yard of our house there on Juniper. And they pulled the thing back and had me aimed straight for the moon. I was in line to beat Armstrong by a good eight years. I would have been not just the youngest person on the moon, but the very first. You could have been reading about me in your history books. There's no doubt that you *would have been*, in fact, were it not for one factor.

Vivian Rowe.

Vivian Rowe lived next door. We were closed in pretty nicely there on Juniper for all of those growing up years, with Uncle Angus and Bounce next door guarding the north border and Vivian and her sweet daughter Faye (the one Coca-Cola and I called "Flip") guarding the south. Plus we all met together three times a week for church, about four blocks away.

I guess I always was crazy about Vivian. I'm sure there would be many reasons we bonded, but what she did that day didn't do anything to hurt. She was a good neighbor and a good lady, too. Of all the years I knew her, I only saw one little-bitty fault in her:

She was nosier than anything you've ever seen.

Didn't anything happen around that part of Juniper Street that she didn't know about, especially over in our direction.

And I must say that, while some found that quality to be a bit overbearing, it was one that I found to be refreshing. You see, because Vivian Rowe was nosy and always looking out her window to see what in the Sam Hill was going on next door, she spotted Tim and Wayne when they tied me to the limb of that Chinaberry tree. And she saw them pull it back and turn it just right so that I was on a perfect lunar navigational path. She saw it soon enough that she was able to grab her broom and head out her back door hollering and screaming for those boys to "let that lil' boy down and please Lord don't let go of that limb."

Vivian Rowe came to my rescue just in the nick of time. I was seconds away from a rough moon landing, but my wonderful little five-foot-tall neighbor who grew to be like a mama to me gave me a few more years to live and love.

I'm pretty thankful for that, too.

Those who know me best know that I may do some strange things every now and then, but those things pale in comparison to what I would have been doing if those two brothers of mine had let go of that tree limb.

I couldn't even have told you all of these stories, because I'm pretty sure they don't have typewriters on the moon.

July 7, 2001

Inspiration Point #23

At any moment we could pause and make a list of complaints that would fill a Sears and Roe-buck Catalog. With about the same energy, we could count a hundred blessings that have come our way—100 inspiration points!

ONE HUNDRED AND ONE REASONS TO BE HAPPY!

 W hat makes *you* happy?…

Think about that.

I had the chance to ask some young people that question recently when some of them forgot to do a little assignment. In looking for a creative way to make 'em pay and learn at the same time, I got an idea: In addition to making them do the assignment they missed, for "interest," I had them write a list of 101 reasons to be happy.

I got some doosies in return.

Chickens.

Cheap horror movies.

Breathing

Bladders (bladders???).

And my all-time favorite: toilet paper.

So I thought maybe *you* need a reminder of a few reasons for us to be happy, so here's my list of one hundred and one. Buckle your seatbelt and see where it takes us…

Writing a column every week—and knowing that

you're reading it, too—seeing kids' faces light up when you bring them candy, students hollering "Hey, Coach!" across the parking lot, and hearing the bell ring at 3:45 that says it's time to let school out for the day.

Peanut butter, whipped cream, strawberries, chocolate, and Mexican food. (Unfortunately, those last two are not on my diet.)

Hearing "I love you" and saying it, too (it's only a happy thing *after* saying it, because it can be torture getting it to come out), hearing somebody say, "You're right" (especially when they doubted it), saying "Good morning, ladies and gentlemen" four times a day to start my classes, and saying "You know you're my favorite niece" to any one of several nieces I have.

Sunsets, sunrises, walking on the beach, beautiful paintings, and eagles flying high in the sky.

Getting poetic right out of the blue, getting sentimental, too; making people laugh, making 'em cry, and making 'em say, "I wonder what he'll say next."

Seeing pictures of my two kiddos when they were young, hearing Rachel tell me about her school adventures on the phone, giving Mal advice that I know he'll take down the road four or five years, embarrassing them when we're out in public, and aggravating them in their 20s the way I did when they were two.

Smiling, laughing, daydreaming, sleeping, and praying.

Having a friend named Jesus, knowing He's the world's greatest forgiver, reminding Him each day that I'm going to need Him to be on "high alert" throughout the day in case I take the wrong road, asking my good Friend to lead wherever He wants me to go, and thanking Him for taking an interest in somebody as faulty and high-maintenance as me.

Influences of the past and present: Mama, Preacher Miller, Grandma, the little blonde who said "I do" thirty years ago but didn't know what all that entailed (the one I jokingly tell my students at school is the luckiest woman in the world), and my red-headed Georgian Uncle Alton and his wife (and Mama's little sister) Aunt Florence, who think of me kind of like their own.

Coca-Cola Mike, Bathtub Steve, Glory and Lee Ann, and Uncle Angus—even though the only one of the bunch who would've appreciated having his name in this book would've been Uncle Angus, if he could have lived to see it.

Poetry, funny stories, motivational stories, inspirational quotes, and Bible stories.

Caleb, Joshua, Abraham, Joseph, and the apostle who always found a way to put his foot in his mouth (ah, you remember Simon Peter!).

Psalm 23 and Psalm 103, 1 Samuel 16:7, the book of Philippians, and my favorite Bible verse of all, Isaiah 40:31.

Singing, telling Bible stories, telling funny stories, going to church, and hearing the preacher say "In conclusion" when he gets a bit long-winded.

Basketball, popcorn, exercising, reading the sports page, and eating hotdogs at the ballpark.

Mark Twain, Lewis Grizzard, Huck Finn, Harper Lee, the Statler Brothers, and my friend Doosey with all his missing teeth.

The Smoky Mountains, "Welcome To Georgia," "La Grange City Limits," tall pine trees, and red clay.

"Support Your Local Sheriff," "Hoosiers, " "Fried Green Tomatoes," "Remember the Titans," and "Pistol."

"Amazing Grace," "How Beautiful Heaven Must Be," "I'm On My Way," "Gloryland Way," and "You Ain't

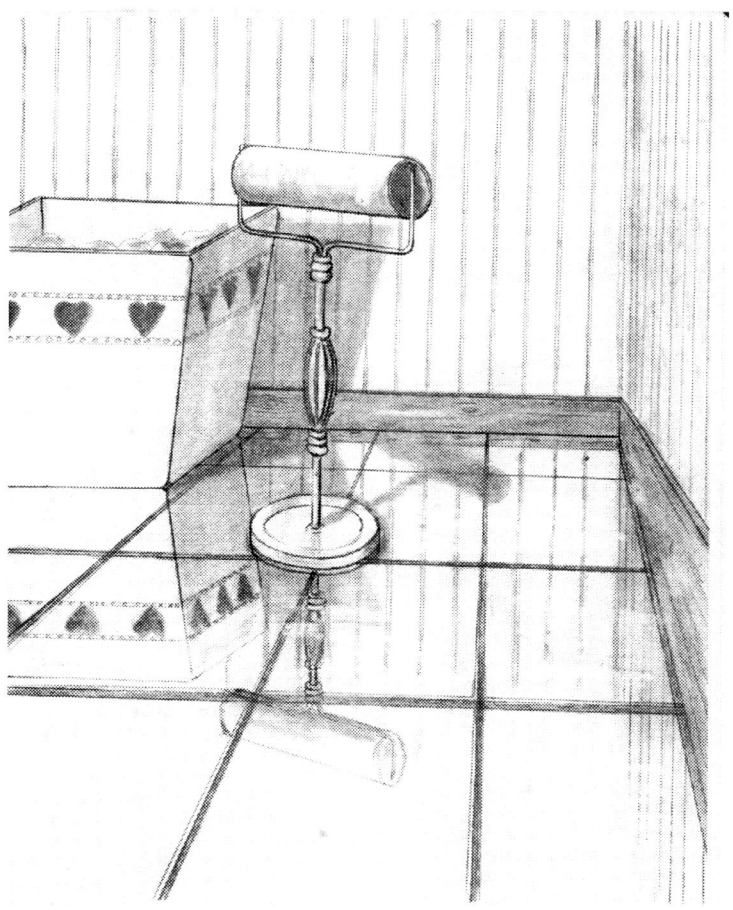

#101: Toilet paper.

Nothin' but a Hound Dog."

Nearing the end of an article, wrapping it up and sending it off, getting notes and e-mails from my readers, and getting a check in the mail.

I believe that's 100, and I need one more, but my mind

has gone blank, right there one shy of 101. I guess I'll have to borrow one from one of my students, if it's all the same.

And toilet paper.

April 26, 2003

Oops, one more thing...

I mentioned Doosey as one of my one hundred and one reasons to be happy. I'd better pause right here and say a word about him, or else he may come looking for me. If you know Doosey—the big fella with the webbed right hand and attitude problem—you know that wouldn't be too happy of a thing at all.

So, Doosey, I want to offer you this apology:

Sorry I didn't get a story about you in this edition of *Inspiration Point*. It sure isn't because you didn't inspire me, because you did that many times over on that brick job in Roanoke, Alabama.

You remember.

Putting your webbed hand over your heart right in the middle of laying brick and telling me all the right things to say to the girls.

Telling me how rich I was going to be when I convinced that one particular young lady to convince her daddy to add my name to the inheritance—things like that.

I needed that back then, when I was sixteen. It was good stuff for me to hear, even though I knew you never told a girl any of those things yourself. Or maybe you did. That might explain all of your missing teeth.

But all of the hikers on this particular trip up to the Point will want to hear all about your stories, so next time around I'll make sure I get you in. I would've written more about you this time, but I had already sent the book in to the publisher when I remembered.

Inspiration Point #24

One of the most inspiring moments I've ever felt occurs each New Year's Eve the last hour of the year. Many folks around the world celebrate with champagne and "Auld Lang Syne." But I get to do better. I get to celebrate with the "Rock of Ages"...

"ROCK OF AGES" THE BEST PART OF ALL

EXcitement has filled the air every New Year's Eve for as long as I can remember.

It's not balloons and horns sounding and "Auld Lang Syne" and kissing.

It's something better.

It's the singing of "Rock of Ages"…

I'm reminded of this inspirational moment every New Year's when I—along with a thousand others—go up to Oklahoma City for a church meeting similar to the one in Sulphur, Oklahoma, except this one is often accompanied by snow and ice while Sulphur's trademark is heat and sweat.

Still, folks come from all over just the same to get a glimpse of what heaven must be like with all the preaching and singing. Those thousand folks—coming all the way from the deep South to the west coast—will congregate in a high school auditorium there in Oklahoma City the last few days before the old year reluctantly passes the banner on to the new. With so many people there, it's a fine chance to see people you only see a couple times a year.

That renewal of old acquaintances is a nice part of the meeting, but it's not the best part.

You'll also get a chance to hear a fella named Lynwood preach, should you happen up there for the meeting one year. Lynwood is in charge of the meeting and has been for most of the fifty years the meeting has been going on. Without a doubt, he's the best storyteller I've ever heard. He can describe a scene better than Huck Finn, such as that wayward prodigal boy headed home to his father with his father coming out to meet him. He draws the picture so well that you're bound to see the smile on the father's face from way off and the dust on the boy's feet, all at the same time.

Naturally, he takes every opportunity he can to say a few words and dip down into his deep well of nostalgia (he's in his seventies now, so that well is plenty deep). If you need some inspiration, Lynwood could supply about a year's worth right there in Oklahoma at the end of the year.

But, still, that's not the best part.

One of the most inspiring scenes you've ever seen occurs at about 11:30 on New Year's Eve. Everybody gathers in the auditorium for the last time during the meeting and for the last time of the year, and a friend of Lynwood's named Johnny Elmore leads the singing of just about every old hymn you can think of. The Elmores are well known for their singing ability, but—in my way of thinking—Johnny is the best of all. Lynwood sometimes calls him the "sweet singer of Israel," and for good reason, too. On that last night at 11:30, Johnny will lead the thousand plus crowd in singing those old hymns—and it's all done a cappella, of course.

One by one, a gentleman from the crowd will suggest a good old hymn he'd like to hear, and Johnny will lead it and those thousand tongues will fill the air with the most inspirational sound you can imagine. If the apostle Paul himself could attend, I imagine he'd say that the singing is so beautiful that it's not lawful to utter it.

But, still, the best part is yet to come.

About five minutes before the bell tolls midnight, Lynwood will look back a moment to the past, reflecting on the victories and defeats, just like it was with the children of Israel. If you can listen to him get nostalgic that way— with his seventy-plus years back in his rearview mirror— without a little tear popping up in your eye, then you're a bigger man than I am.

But even that's not the best part.

At 11:59, Lynwood will pass the baton back to Johnny who'll lead the people in a final song to sing the old year out and the new one in. The crowd, sometimes with choked voices and always with blurry eyes, will blend their voices to perhaps the grandest old song of them all, and in so doing will usher in another year full of victories and defeats, and joy and sorrow, all the things that a new year brings with it.

I bet you've sung that old song yourself a time or two:

Rock of Ages, cleft for me, let me hide myself in Thee. Let the water and the blood, from Thy wounded side which flowed. Be of sin, the double cure. Save from wrath, and make me pure...

And now you know the best part of all.

January 5, 1998

Inspiration Point #25

I promised you a few more moments at
Grandma's before we head back down. After the
angels came and we all told her goodbye in our
final visit to her home, I felt something was
missing. It took awhile before I figured out what
it was, because conducting the celebration of
Grandma's life was the most important business
at hand. But before heading back west, I walked
into Grandma's house as I'd done a thousand
times, and I found myself alone for the first
time—just me and Grandma…I'd be honored if
you'd join me there…

SPENDING A LITTLE TIME ALONE WITH GRANDMA, AGAIN

Ah, Yes! I stood in Grandma's house the other day—just the two of us—very much like before.

Almost.

It was the day that we had walked with her as far as we are allowed to walk on this side of heaven.

The one thing I had missed most about the trip to Grandma's was that I wasn't able to spend time with her the way I always had. She had gone on, and the task at hand was to greet friends and family and to prepare the best thoughts I knew to say when we all came together to celebrate her life.

All of those things were good—but it wasn't like spending time alone with Grandma in Grandma's house.

So on the evening after it was all said and done, some of the family gathered at the house that Grandma had spent a lifetime making a home—or, better yet, at the home Grandma had spent a lifetime making a little like heaven.

But as the time drew nearer to make our way back west, I felt an emptiness. Something was missing.

I didn't really know what it was, because the fatigue of driving all night—along with saying goodbye to one of the few angels I know—had everything a little jumbled inside.

It dawned on me what it was when the family drifted out to the front porch and visited, and I walked inside the house—alone.

For the first time on the trip, it was just me—and Grandma.

That was what I needed.

I stood for a long time, watching Grandma do what she always did.

Fixing the cornbread and putting it in the oven.

Making "a taste of red velvet cake" (my favorite), because she'd promised she'd make one before I had to go back.

Shucking some corn that Brother Ivy Thompson had brought her from his garden.

"We'll have that corn for supper," Grandma said, "along with some fresh onion and green beans that Ivy picked for us. And, of course," she added, "we'll have some good buttermilk to go with the hot cornbread."

"That sounds good, Grandma," I said. "I'm hungry already."

So she worked on, as always—smoothly, majestically, painlessly, lovingly, tirelessly, joyfully.

I watched her in admiration, as I had done hundreds of times. She was working to make my stay that of a king. There was no pain she wasn't willing to take. I was her king, and her work in the kitchen was her way of putting a purple robe on me and a ring on my hand and shoes on my feet.

She wasn't standing in the kitchen with her hands covered with flour and her heart covered in love.

I never felt better than I felt when I was with Grandma.

So I had to watch her one more time, had to be with her just for a little while before I left town. Unlike all the other times, when I left, I knew there would be no more coming home to Grandma.

So, with a smile and a tear, I stood and watched her work, soaking it all in.

Then, when she paused to rest her tired legs, I gathered our clothes and began packing the car—ah, just as before!

All the times before, I'd always grit my teeth and hope that Grandma would be there when—in a few months—life's demands could be laid aside long enough for me to come home again.

But this time—when the stay was ended and the packed car pulled out of heaven's driveway—it was different. Grandma wouldn't be there to give that final hug, and she wouldn't be able to say "I love you" a little bashfully.

Not this time.

She wasn't standing in the kitchen with her hands covered with flour and her heart covered in love.

Still, she was very much alive—down deep in the aching recesses of this young boy's heart.

As I drove away from Grandma's this final time and headed west, I knew that's where she'd stay.

October 18, 2003

Inspiration Point #26

All right, good friends: Thanks for staying with me 'til the end and sharing those final moments at Grandma's house. That was special. We've come full circle, now, here in *Inspiration Point,* back to Bromide Hill. Sulphur, Oklahoma, still holds great memories, along with that hill out-side of town. But the young folks have started a new tradition up on Bromide. Actually, I started it a long time ago, and they never even knew it. They also don't know that I could've told them that this new fad doesn't work up there. At least, it never did for me back in the '70s…

BROMIDE HILL NOT THE PLACE FOR PRAYER

Zealous boys looking for a girl and zealous preachers looking for a sermon still arrive in Sulphur, Oklahoma, around July 4…

They've been doing that since long before I was born, and—as you know—I wasn't born yesterday.

They come from all over the country—from the orange groves of California all the way to the peach groves of Georgia—to get the feel of a big-time revival in a cozy mountainous town in the middle of Oklahoma.

What you get at Sulphur is all-you-can-handle gospel preaching and singing, almost completely out in the open for the world to see. I say "almost" because the services are conducted under a big building, but the sides are let up, and some people sit in lawn chairs on the outside so as not to keep the beautiful harmony of a thousand a cappella voices all to themselves.

It's quite a scene.

As heavenly as that scene is—and I have to say it's

one of the best scenes I've ever been a part of—there's more to Sulphur than that, especially if you're a youngster in your dating years. In fact, if a fella happened to be down on his luck in the dating department, Sulphur would definitely be the place to go with the mission of "I'm gonna find me a wife before I leave if it's the last thing I do." Some have found wives that way, and I guess a few have died trying.

After all the singing and preaching is concluded, all the boys scramble around to try to find a date to take out to one of the church activities and then maybe to a scenic area afterwards to look at the stars.

That brings me again to that one special spot: Bromide Hill. There she sits still, one of the highest hills on top of the Arbuckle Mountains, overlooking Sulphur and the surrounding cities. She sits up there majestically, admiring what looks like a thousand specks of lights scattered for miles around. I guess one of the prettiest sights that I ever remember is looking over the city from Bromide Hill on a dark night with the stars shining ever so bright.

The stars up in the sky weren't the only ones you could see, either, because if you had the right girl and could sneak a little kiss at the conclusion of some well-timed poetry, you could see other stars that'd make the ones up above tip their hat in appreciation.

I've already told you about that.

That's the way it's been for as long as I can remember.

But there's something I haven't told you. Something *has* changed about Sulphur.

When I arrived at the church service not long ago, I ran into my teenage buddy Sethie from Red Oak, Texas, who was at Sulphur with his newfound love, Lindsey. (Lindsey is one of those who came all the way from the orange groves of California.)

Just to make sure I gave him the benefit of my vast experience in this area, I asked him right off the bat if he were planning on taking Lindsey up to Bromide Hill.

"Aw, yeah, Coach," he said, "we go every year."

That really surprised me, because I never remember his asking me to dip into my encyclopedia of knowledge to give him a few tips. I'm sure he just forgot.

"Oh," I said, trying to hide my surprise, "how do ya'll, uh, like it up on Bromide?"

"Aw, Coach," he said, "it's one of the neatest things. A few couples go up there late at night on July 3, and we all hold hands in a circle and pray."

When I heard that, for a moment I saw some of those stars that I used to see up on Bromide back thirty years ago.

Pray?! They go to Bromide Hill and pray! I couldn't believe it. What's becoming of this young generation?

I really admire Sethie and Lindsey and the young kids who have elevated this great scene to a loftier spiritual level. I didn't want to burst their bubble, so I didn't tell them what I'm about to tell you. I just told them I admired them and that I really hoped they'd have a good time. But I couldn't help shaking my head a little as I walked away.

What I didn't tell them was that praying doesn't work on Bromide.

You see, I tried praying up there once, back in the 1970s. And, as far as I could tell, it just didn't seem to be the best spot for the activity.

I had a date one night with one of the prettiest girls ever to put on a long, beautiful flowery dress and a matching hat. I took her up to Bromide, and the whole time I was quoting poetry to her, I was praying that before the night was over I could sneak a little kiss.

*I was praying that before the night was over I could sneak
a little kiss.*

I must have been in rare poetic form that night, because every time I leaned over to get an answer to my prayer, she laughed and told me to stop it.

"Quote me another poem," she'd say.

So, I did a lot of praying that night up on Bromide Hill, but I'm sorry to say I never got one of them answered. The only good news is that I did quote thirty-seven poems before the night was through, even a few I made up on the spot.

July 4, 2003

As we head back down the hill…
I've got to share one more
Inspirational Point!

A ways back on our little journey, I promised you I'd give you a preview of a future hike up Inspiration Point.

We've traveled *back* for the most part on this trip, and it's always inspirational to me to remember what Mama and Grandma and Preacher Miller and others offered. Their inspiration lasts a lifetime.

Then, in February, 2005, something amazing hit me. I had become a grandfather myself (Okay, a *young* one, but still a grandfather!) How could I ever hope to inspire my grandson the way my grandparents inspired me?

I don't know if that's possible, but I know I have a great pattern. You can't beat that.

So, a few months before Connor Reed Osburn was born—the lad I call my little Dewey—I sat down and wrote him a letter. That time of reflection was like looking down over Sulphur, Oklahoma, from a rock at the top of Bromide Hill. But when I would hold the young fella for the first time a few months later, I about fell off the mountain!

I'll hope to share all of that with you—and much more—when we take this journey again. For now, I'll share the first letter, written *almost* from the peak of Bromide Hill. He wasn't quite born yet, but for me it was a classic trip to Inspiration Point.

GRANDSON TO LEAD NEXT TRIP UP INSPIRATION POINT!

Dear Little Dewey,

Wow!

That's the best way I know to begin my first ever letter to my best and most special friend.

I can't believe, son, that you're well on your way. Before long, I'm going to be teaching you everything I know. Okay, some may think that won't take but a couple of minutes, but I'm going to try to learn as much as I can between now and the time you walk on stage so I can prepare you to face all of life's little challenges.

You may think this is a little funny, but—as I write this very special letter—you are still a little fella in your mama's tummy. You won't be catching that Greyhound out to the real world for another five months. Right now, the good Lord is forming you in a marvelous way. It's like the psalmist said a long time ago, you are being amazingly and wonderfully made. Right this minute the good Lord is counting those toes to make sure they're five—on each foot, that is—and counting those fingers, and arranging your lungs and liver nice and neat where they go, and making sure your head is the right size, although when I get through with you it might be a tad bigger than it needs to be. And more than that, he's planning out all the great things in life you're going to be able to do. Isn't that amazing?!

Now, little one, even though you think I'm pretty smart, all of that is just a little too much for me. But I think the Lord does kind of like what I'm doing right now. I'm making some plans for you, too, and for us. And they're the biggest and best plans I know how to make.

But don't you worry about those things now. Right now, you just worry about breathing in and out—imagining you're up in the mountains of Colorado or somewhere where the air is clean and fresh—and you just make sure you grab as much good food as you can while you're growing there in your little world. Every now and then it'll be all right if you give Mama a swift kick, just to let her know that when the Greyhound pulls into the station, you're going to be hitting the ground a-runnin'.

Back to some of the things I'm going to have to teach you: I have a few things in mind, but I may need more time to think. Remember, I just learned today that you are a little boy, so my imagination has just now shifted into high gear. But I do have a few things in mind.

I know I want to teach you how to play basketball. Aw, little Dewey, I'm gonna have to teach you how to make one of those down-low, quick, stop-ya-in-ya-tracks crossover moves. And, of course, I'll show you my specialty, the long-range three-point shot. Don't worry. I'm going to keep myself in good shape so I'll be able to do all of those things. I'll hit the track as often as I can, and I'll devote quite a bit of time working on all my moves in the gym, because—by the time you're three or four years old—you're going to need a good sparring partner. I'm the man for that job.

Aw, Dewey, you'd better get ready to learn, because we have a lot of things to cover. Basketball is great and will give you and me and your mama some good times, because she loves basketball, too. But I want you to know that the most important thing I'm going to teach you is about the Lord.

The Lord, son, is going to make you quite a gentleman. He's probably going to give you some of your dad's Clint-Eastwood toughness, your mom's big heart, your Grandma's sense of family, and a little bit of my style. Why, he'll probably even make you a great preacher. Still—to my way of thinking—it never hurts for a tough, big-hearted, family-man preacher with all kinds of style to have a take-ya-breath-away jump shot.

Oh, yeah, Dewey—about your name. Your name isn't really Dewey. I thought you should know that. Your mama and daddy are thinking about calling you something like Connor Reed. But they're not sure.

So, while they're making up their minds—and maybe for the next forty or fifty years—I think I'll just call you my little Dewey, although in front of them I may have to go with the more formal Connor or Conner Reed, just to keep the peace.

For me, just call me Coach. Or—to make your mama and grandma happy—"Pop" will do just fine, too.

And always know this, little one, as I tell it to you for the first time.

I really love you, even though we haven't met just yet.

Pop

POST-WARNING

So, there you have it.

You can't say you weren't warned beforehand.

I told you the stories would make you cry, and then sometimes they'd make you laugh—at the same time. I know it's true, because that's what they did for me.

These were stories of the Southland, back-home stories that remind us of the way it was and—I guess—of the way it still is way down deep.

When the stories of "way-back" come to mind, they remind us of a hundred key points along the way that mold and touch and change and inspire us.

I don't know how to describe such a point in a life, except to call it what we've called it here:

Inspiration Point.

Thank you for hiking up to Inspiration Point with me. Stay in shape, because I look forward for us to do it again soon!

*I don't know how to describe it, except to call it
Inspiration Point!*

A SPECIAL INVITATION

It is a great privilege that I have to share inspirational and motivational thoughts and stories to thousands of readers through newspaper columns as well as through books.

If the Lord's willing, I have many other books to write, and I hope that you'll be able to come along with me on those journeys, too.

But with the blessing to write comes a great responsibility. As you've seen, I've shared much of my faith in the pages of *Inspiration Point*. I know that among the many thousands who have graciously bought and read this book, many of you will not know Jesus Christ. I would not feel this book would be complete if I did not include an invitation for you to know Him, because He will make all the difference in your life.

Sometimes, too, good people *think* they know him, but they are misled by human reasoning, and I want to make sure that is not the case with you.

The final word in our journey together is a sharing of the simple gospel plan of salvation. What you'll read here is not what you're likely to hear on television, because many leave out parts that the Lord puts in. The Lord's plan of salvation can be seen in simple form in one story over in the book of Acts.

I love this old story. It's the story of the eunuch of Acts 8 who was riding along in a chariot reading the scriptures when the Lord sent the evangelist Philip to him. This eunuch had some special qualities about him. He had a passion to know God's Word, and he had an open heart.

When Philip came up to the eunuch as he read, Philip asked him if he understood what he was reading. The eunuch replied,

"How can I, except some man should guide me?"

The good man was searching for truth, but he just couldn't understand it. He needed help.

For many miles in that old chariot, Philip rode along with him and shared with him the gospel of Jesus.

It's kind of like what we're doing right here.

Philip began right there in the fifty-third chapter of Isaiah and, in the words of the writer Luke, "preached to him Jesus" (verse 35).

The nobleman from Ethiopia perhaps had heard of Jesus, but he didn't know Him. But that journey from Jerusalem to Ethiopia would be his greatest journey, because that day he would hear and he would learn the greatest story ever told!

After Philip preached Jesus to him for many miles, they came to a little pool of water. The eunuch—perhaps raising his hand to get Philip to pause—said to the evangelist,

"Look. Here's water. Why can't I be baptized?"

As those wheels had been turning on the chariot, Philip, in preaching Jesus, had preached water baptism to the unbelieving nobleman.

Philip said, "You can, if you believe in Jesus Christ with all your heart!"

The nobleman, his heart bursting with excitement, made this great confession. I believe they are the greatest words a man can utter:

He said, "I believe that Jesus Christ is the son of God!" (Acts 8:37).

Upon his newfound faith in Jesus and his confession of the same, Philip and the eunuch went down into the water, and Philip baptized him.Ah, what an inspirational point that was for the Ethiopian nobleman. No wonder he went on his way rejoicing! (verse 39).

He had fulfilled the words of Jesus Himself, who instructed the disciples before he ascended back to heaven, "He that believes and is baptized shall be saved!" (Mark 16:16). What cause for rejoicing!

In a simple story in inspired scripture we have a picture of a man's salvation. There are others, too (Acts 2:37-38; Acts 22:16; Acts 16:14-15, 29-34), that show us how to act upon our faith in order to be saved.

As I told you early on in our journey, Preacher Miller took me down to the water when I was just a boy. I've never been the same.

I've witnessed many others through the years confess their faith in the Lord and surrender to the Lord in baptism, as well. I've even been privileged to assist a few in that great act. It's quite a scene to watch or assist a sinner as he is "buried in baptism" (Romans 6:3-4). It's inspiring, too, to see the tears on the faces of the new Christian and his family as their hearts overflow!

There are no greater inspiration points than those.

The Lord's invitation is the most powerful one you'll

ever receive. If you haven't responded to it, please do it now.

Contact me, and I'll be glad to guide you as best I can, just as Philip guided the nobleman.

May God bless you all!

Again, thanks for putting on your hiking boots. It's been quite a journey!

Steven

ABOUT THIS SOUTHERN WRITER

Steven Ray Bowen was born and raised in La Grange, Georgia in 1956 and from day one was shaped by almost bigger-than-life figures: his grandfather E.H. Miller, his grandma (Zona Belle Miller), and, of course, his mama Fanny Louise Bowen.

Their stories are told in part in *Inspiration Point.*

Steven's mama ended her journey in October of 1973, and that departure would take him away, too—from the red clay he'd always known to the black-land dirt of Texas. But he carried that deep-South influence with him as he and his red 1965 Chevy Nova headed west.

In 1975—two years after leaving Georgia—Steven married Marilyn Dickinson from Houston, and they have two children: Rachel Louise—a dedicated 3rd-grade teacher in Houston— born in 1977, and Steven Malachi (Mal)—a chaser of dreams kind of like his dad—born in 1980. Rachel provided Steven his first grandson Connor Reed Osburn in February 2005.

After working for ten years as a bricklayer to get through school, Steven graduated from the University of

Houston in 1984 and received a M.A. in Literature from UH at Clear Lake in 1989. For twenty-two years he has taught English and—for the past eight—a motivational speech class that he loves.

Two other of Steven's passions are coaching basketball—which he's done for twenty-two years in five different Texas high schools—and sharing the gospel of Jesus Christ, which he has been privileged to do both in writing and preaching for most of his life.

Steven wrote his first book in 1989, an unpublished novel called *Crossing the Georgia Line.* He published his first book in 1997, a Southern humor book called *That Southern Red Clay Jus' Won't Wash Off.* In the same year, he began writing his weekly humor/inspirational newspaper column for his hometown of La Grange, Georgia. He now writes weekly for several papers in Georgia, Alabama, and Texas.

ORDERING AND CONTACT INFORMATION

Steven Bowen is the author of the following books:

That Southern Red Clay Jus' Won't Wash Off
Inspiration Point

To order *Inspiration Point*, send $14 to:

Steven Bowen
P.O. Box 2125
Red Oak, Texas 75154

(Include $1.50 for shipping and handling *per order*)

Or contact Steven for more information:
e-mail: steven.bowen@redoakisd.org
phone: 972-824-5197

You also may contact *Inspiration Point's* excellent artist, Steve Smith, at ssmith10253@cox.net.

Printed in the United States
81783LV00001B